A NOVEL BY
AVERY GOODE

COPYRIGHT

SPECIAL THANK YOU'S

Always first and foremost, Jesus I thank you. It's in You that I live, move and have my being. All my witty, creative and ORIGINAL ideas come from You. Thank You so much for this gift and for giving me the opportunity to share it with the world.

To my love bugs; Kenisha, Tory and Tarez, Jah'vyon, Azauriah, JaLynn, Brooklynn, Sincere and Deion you all keep me motivated and encouraged. You make me believe I can do any and everything and support me through it all. I love you all.

Mama, Toots, Keesha, Tranique, Tristan, Tre'on, TJ, Zion...Your support is priceless and your love never-ending.

To all family who support me, Tammy and the Elite 8, Mrs. Joyce and Mr. Jeff Dickerson, and Pastor Donald D. Woody, Sr. and the JCA Family.

Vanessa Mapp-Andell James, Jonathyn, Nikki Covil, Bonita Gipson, Thonie Lee and Tonya Pickett, Susan Fox, Danyelle Cooksey and Tiffany Mason, Avis, Levia, Camille, Antwan Floyd, LaTasha Chappell, Deronda...you all are friends worth having.

Lamont Gilbert, my male counterpart...you are hands down my #1 fan and I love you dude. We've been rocking since Best Buy Auto and will keep on till we're old and gray.

To my Daniel's family who loved us through some difficult times. Please know that we look forward to every time we come together and cherish every memory. Randi, Shawn, Linda, Redd, Jacqui, Lil Man, Covonte, Brandon, Jasmine, Lil Shawn, Antwone and Jack....you're the best extended family a girl could ask for.

Writing would be worthless without my wonderful readers to share it with. Having said that, THANK YOU SO MUCH to every person who has supported me. Every book club who has read my books and every bookstore that has carried them. Whether you borrowed my books, read them in a library, reviewed them, offered me constructive feedback or moral support,

I count it all a blessing. I'm sure that I have left so many wonderful people out but know this, I'm grateful to everyone who has helped me along this journey. Thank you all again and please keep in touch with me.

FB: Avery Good
Twitter: thegoodescribe
IG: thegoodescribe
Periscope: thegoodescribe
Snap: SheGoode
E/M: averygoode@hotmail.com

DEDICATIONS

This book is dedicated to the freak in you...Yes, YOU!
Remember...have fun, be safe, be Goode or be Goode at it. –
AG

PROLOGUE

Pain coursed through her body. It felt as if someone was ripping her insides out using a pair of wire pliers. This baby was giving her as much pain in delivery as he had during her entire pregnancy. Her entire *unwanted* pregnancy. Before the next pain shot through her body, Karen Hudson blacked out, leaving her husband feeling as helpless as he had when all of this first began. Rubbing his wife's hand, Kyle recalled when they first met, and despite his sadness, he smiled.

From the time that Karen Giles walked through the doors at Douglas High School in Atlanta, Georgia and Kyle Hudson laid eyes on her, he felt that he wanted to be with her for the rest of his life. When Karen saw Kyle, he piqued her interest as well, but she didn't tell him. It was love at first sight but neither of them were brave enough to act on it. Kyle was as smooth as a baby's bottom when speaking with young ladies but every time he got near Karen he got tongue-tied.

During his freshman year, Kyle, never managed to get up the nerve to talk to his dream girl but his sophomore year was a different story. Kyle emerged a taller, more confident guy who was not afraid to go after what he wanted. He was also the Raiders basketball team starting forward and hoped his new status was going to help him win Karen over. But three days after school began, Kyle hadn't seen her.

"Man, I don't know why you didn't try harder over the summer to get at her. Now, it doesn't even look like she's coming back to this school," Kyle's best friend, James said.

"I know. I think I screwed up big time with this one. I don't know why I thought that she was going to be returning. Especially knowing that her father is in the military. Fuck, man.

7

I hoped she was going to be my woman for the rest of my life."

"Yo, you too young to be thinking about the rest of your life. Your ass isn't even seventeen yet."

"I know. But Karen was different. She was a lot like my mom only nicer. The kind of chick you took to junior *and* senior prom," Kyle looked off into space.

"Check it out, dude. Granny said if you love something let it go, if it comes back to you, then it was meant for you. If it doesn't, you don't need it."

"I swear James, your grandmother says some of the craziest shit but I can dig it."

"You got that right. Now let's get to this court before it gets too packed with those old heads. You know how those cats like to hog the court." When Kyle didn't reply immediately, James continued. "Man, you'll see her again. One day the foxy lady of your dreams will walk right up on you and the two of you will live happily ever after."

"Whatever man. Come on so I can serve you this Wilt Chamberlain style ass whooping on the court. You're gonna be Walt Frazier."

The two friends left school and went to the recreation center where they met up with some others and played a few games of basketball. Although Kyle played well, his head wasn't all the way in the game. He was praying for that 'one day' to be soon. He had no clue it was going to be a lot sooner than he thought. The weekend flew by and before Kyle knew it, Monday had arrived. This was going to be the first full week of school. Grudgingly, he got out of bed and began preparing for school.

"Kyle, hurry your butt up before you're late for school," his mother called out.

When he came downstairs the first thing his mother noticed was the long face her oldest son wore. Mistakenly, she thought it was because he didn't want to attend school and said something about it.

"School just started back and you already don't want to go? Boy, you betta pick your chin up off the floor and get it together before your daddy gets in here. You know he don't play when it comes to y'alls schooling."

"It's not that Ma. I'm mad at myself because I met a cool person last year and kind of got a big crush on her but I was too tongue-tied to talk to her. I assumed she'd be back this year but she's not."

"You? Tongue-tied? Boy, she must be awfully special to make Mr. Smooth trip over his words."

"Yeah, Ma. She really was. But I missed my chance. Anyway, I got to go. Tell Pops I'll cut the grass when I come home. I love you," Kyle said before kissing his mother on her cheek.

"I love you too, Son. Cheer up though. Good things are in store for you today. My spirit says so."

And she was right. When Kyle made it to his second period class he was so deep in thought that he was oblivious to the new student who was sitting behind him. Had it not been for the teacher calling on her, Kyle would not have paid much attention to the girl at all.

"Quiet down students. We have a late arrival to our roster. She and her parents were in Paris, France so she missed the first few days of school. Karen, will you please come forward and regale us with your vacation tales?" The teacher asked.

Kyle almost fell out of his seat when Karen Giles walked past him. She smelled like fresh roses and vanilla. Exactly as he remembered. He didn't hear a thing she said even though he was staring directly in her mouth.

While Karen was at the front of the class she couldn't help but to focus on Kyle. She didn't take her eyes off him the entire time she spoke. He had gotten a few inches taller and his muscles had developed a little more. He had a great physique as a freshman but he was even sexier to her now. She couldn't wait to return to school so that she could finally tell him everything she really wanted to say since last school term. Neither of them knew that they wanted to tell the other the exact same things. When the bell rang ending the class, Kyle lingered to wait for Karen. She was leaning down gathering her books when he turned around, stood her straight up and kissed her hard on her mouth.

"I'm sorry, Karen but I've wanted to do that since last year," he apologized.

"No need to be sorry, I've wanted you to do that since last year," she admitted.

"Look, I know that you've probably heard some things about me being all smooth and shit with the ladies but when it came to you, I was at a loss for words. I tried everything to get at you last year but I messed up. You may think I'm crazy but I thought about you all summer. Hell, you can ask my friends if you don't believe me."

"I do," she whispered.

"Yeah. One day, you're going to say those same words when you agree to become my wife."

From that moment on the two of them were inseparable. Kyle took Karen to both the junior and the senior prom and she attended every one of his basketball games. Unfortunately, a debilitating knee injury ended Kyle's NBA hoop dreams while he was in college but he graduated with honors nevertheless. Both he and Karen attended and graduated from Morris Brown University and they married soon after graduation. Karen, an elementary school teacher, loved her job and the life that she and her attorney husband had carved out for themselves. While they weren't rich, they lived a very comfortable life in Atlanta.

The couple was working very hard to save for their dream home. Kyle took on extra cases and Karen got a part time waitressing gig at a restaurant not too far from his midtown office. By the time he finished at the office, she was off work as well and the two of them usually arrived home within minutes of one another. This worked out for the couple for almost six months.

With all the hours that Kyle had been working, he was beginning to capture the attention of the senior partners. Knowing that a promotion would help him and his wife financially, Kyle was ecstatic when approached about taking on one of the largest cases the firm ever had. But taking this case meant that he would work longer hours. Karen, who was very proud of her husband and understood how much this meant to him, reassured him that she, would be fine.

"Honey, this is something that you have worked so hard for. Go for it. I'll be okay. Trust me. Plus, once you win this case I can quit my second job," she encouraged.

"Baby, you're the best. Everything that I have always wanted, everything that I have always needed is right here in you," Kyle said, placing his hand over his wife's heart.

"You're such an amazing man, Kyle Hudson and I love you infinitely. Take this case and don't worry about me. I never work later than nine most nights and I'll be fine. There's no reason to worry about me, babe."

For the next few weeks, Karen worked as usual, getting off at nine and heading home alone to wait on her husband. She had grown accustomed to her serving position and got friendly with many of the regulars. She loved her job and the tips were great. One man used to come in each night and order the same thing, coffee and apple pie. He never spoke to anyone but Karen and although his tab was fewer than three dollars, he left Karen a twenty-dollar tip. One night one of the young waitresses quit, leaving the two remaining ones to cover the vacant slot and Karen was now getting off an hour later.

"You need to be careful out there, Sugarplum. It's not safe to walk these streets alone at night," her co-worker warned.

"I know, Gayle. Thankfully I park in the same spot and there are lots of cops on that beat so I'm safe. Plus, God is watching over me."

And God wasn't the only one. Unbeknownst to her, she was being followed. The young man who walked slowly behind her did so to ensure that she made it to her car safely. He had been doing this every night for months, shortly after Karen had taken the job. Because she was still beating Kyle home at night, she never told Kyle about the later hours. She felt like she'd be fine. One night Karen was brutally assaulted on her way home from work.

Her Friday had begun normally as it always had. Get to school, give pop quiz, prepare the upcoming weeks' lesson plan, clock out and head to her job at the Midtown Café. But this day there was an event in downtown Atlanta. There was so much traffic and people swarming the midtown area that it was impossible for her to get her usual parking spot so she had to park almost a half mile away.

The restaurant was full and stayed busy from the time that Karen clocked in until she clocked out at ten that night. Kyle had called to check on her and reluctantly she told him that she was going to work later than normal to help with the large crowd. He wasn't pleased, but Kyle saw there wasn't much he could tell Karen that would make her leave her co-workers in a lurch.

"You know how I feel about you walking alone at night. Be aware of your surroundings always and ask the cook if he'll walk you to your car. If he can't, ask him if you can take one of the knives with you for safety. Will you do that for me?"

"Yes, Kyle I will. But you worry too much. There are more cops out on the streets than it was when President Carter came."

"I don't care about Carter. I care about you. Be careful, woman."

"I will man. I love you, Husband."

"I love you more, Wife."

Kyle returned to work with an uneasy feeling in the pit of his stomach but didn't pay much attention to it. When Karen got off work that night, she hugged her good friend, Gayle and left. She didn't ask the cook to walk her to her car nor had she grabbed a knife for protection. Karen didn't think she'd need it. She was wrong. It was darker than usual but

13

Karen wasn't fazed by it. Tired, she decided to take a short cut between some buildings at Tenth and Piedmont thinking it would be quicker than walking around them on her way to her car.

Karen walked at a brisk pace, enjoying the loud music that blasted from the club she passed. Jamming, walking through the alley, Karen was oblivious to the man walking a few steps behind her. He was dressed in all black and blended in with his dark surroundings waiting for the perfect opportunity to act. All he wanted to do was talk to her. For months, she had captivated him and he felt beyond the shadow of a doubt, that he was in love with her. He felt that once she got to know him, she would in turn, love him too.

Almost tripping over her untied shoe lace, Karen stopped long enough to bend down and tie it. The man saw his chance and seized it. He reached out and touched Karen's shoulder after she stood, startling her and she dropped her purse, spilling its contents on the ground.

"Jesus. Look what you made me do. Don't you know better than to sneak up on someone like that?" Karen kneeled to pick up her belongings.

"I'm sorry, My Love. I've wanted to talk to you and never had a chance. I thought I would walk you to your car and we could talk. I want to hear about your day, My Love."

"Please don't call me that. And get away from me, you're scaring me."

"I'm not trying to scare you, My Love. I'm here to protect you as I have done for months. I want to talk to you."

"I'm married and even if I wasn't I wouldn't give you the time of day." Karen regretted it as soon as she uttered those words. She had made an enormous mistake.

His eyes glazed over and even in the dark she could see the evil that lurked behind them.

"Married? But you can't be. You're mine. What kind of husband allows his woman to walk alone at night? You are mine," he stated adamantly. "That's why I have been walking with you. I keep you safe you ungrateful, bitch."

A fearful Karen clutched her bag to her body and tried to move around the man. Before she got past him, he grabbed her arm.

He leaned near her ear and said, "do not scream or I will cut your throat."

The knife pressing lightly against her throat was a promise, not a threat. The man pulled her behind a large dumpster, pushed her down face first onto the ground and began fondling her.

"I don't want to kill you, My Love, but I will. All I wanted to do was love you. But bitches like you don't want that. I thought that you were different from the others. Worthy of my love."

Karen tried to scream.

"Don't scream. Don't move. Don't die."

Before Karen realized what was happening, the man managed to get her panties down and hiked her skirt up. He used his knee to part her legs and his left hand to release his hard dick from his pants. Karen felt her body stretch as the man pushed his thick, long tool inside her dry vagina, causing her to cry out in pain.

"You like that don't you, bitch?" He said as he pounded her mercilessly.

Karen cried silently and prayed that he wouldn't kill her. The man let out a howl as he released his seed inside her. His member went soft but he didn't pull out. Instead, he kissed the back of Karen's neck with rough, chapped lips. His breath reeked of liquor and fish, making Karen sick to her stomach. She tried to scoot from up under him but her slight movement both angered and aroused him at the same time.

He made shallow, one-inch cuts in Karen's back and she tried her hardest not to scream out in pain. The man wiped some of the blood off her and used it to saturate his dick. To further add to her disgust, he licked the warm blood off her body and savored the taste of her. Once he stroked his dick back to life using her blood as lubricant, the man took both hands, while gripping the knife between his teeth, to spread her ass cheeks and shoved his dick into her anus.

The pain of being violated in her backside was more than Karen could bare and she passed out. When she woke up, she was at Emory Hospital where she was told she had been for three days. The look of sadness on her husband's face caused Karen to look away from him in embarrassment and shame.

"Don't turn away from me, Wife. I love you and we will get through this. I'm not going anywhere. I'm with you all the way."

Two months after her sexual assault, Charlie Byron Clark was apprehended on twenty-five counts of rape and twenty-four counts of murder. Karen was the only victim he didn't kill. The only woman who could testify against him when he was finally tried in court. It was her testimony which helped convict him and that led to his sentence of death. He was executed sixteen months after sentencing. Stressed during the trial, Karen paid no attention to the woman who showed up every day and sat at the back of the courtroom. Nor had she realized that she missed her period four months in a row. By the time she realized she was pregnant, it was too late for her to terminate the pregnancy. She had no choice but to have her rapist's baby.

She should have known that all those bouts of vomiting were more than stress. Karen lost so much weight she had to drink Ensure to make sure her body got the nutrition it needed. A few months after her attack, she started throwing up almost daily. Every smell made her sick and she experienced the worst cramps ever. The child was likely to be as evil as the man who had planted the seed inside her. The Hudson's were certain the baby wasn't Kyle's because they had been using protection. They wanted to wait to start a family after he finished the case, hoping it would lead to more money.

When she found out she was pregnant, Karen took the remainder of the school year off because she didn't want anyone to know. Moreover, she didn't want them to ask where the baby was when they didn't see him. She and Kyle had decided to place the child for adoption.

As Kyle rubbed his wife's hand, the memories of how they had gotten to this point brought tears to his eyes. He should have been there for his wife and yet, he had let her down. Now, as the moments drew near for her to rid her body of what she called 'the demon spawn', he feared for her life once again because he felt as if this baby understood exactly what he was doing and was trying to kill her. After twenty hours of the most painful labor, Karen delivered a healthy, yet loud, baby boy. They never saw his face and didn't want to hold him. He wasn't theirs. Their attorney told them that they found a family for the baby before he was ever born. They declined meeting the adoptive family. Happily, she and Kyle signed away their parental rights as the small child was placed with his new family and they never looked back.

Eventually, the couple healed and a few years later, bought their dream home and filled it with five children of their own. The first four births were easy. Kayla was their first daughter; Kyle Jr. was their first and only son and they were eleven months apart. Two years later, Kellie and Kennedi, their twins, popped out. The couple was done having children. But God didn't agree. Two years later, a little girl, made her glorious appearance with much fuss and attitude. Karen perceived this little girl was going to be different from any of her other children because she felt it. Karen wasn't psychic, but she was right on all counts.

WHAT A GIRL WANTS

Kalia Rae Hudson was the brick house The Commodores sang about all those years ago. 36-24-36. She had a body that rivaled that of any grown woman. A body that she wasn't afraid to use. One that she used well. At five feet seven inches tall and one hundred forty-five pounds, Kalia was thick in all the right places. Already a vixen, she was a force to be reckoned with. Long, thick, straight, black hair; milk chocolate skin; hazel brown eyes. She looked like her new favorite actress, Maia Campbell from the hit show, In the House with LL Cool J. And she wasn't even grown yet.

Pretty as a picture and smart as a whip, Kalia thought she had it going on. Even though Atlanta was the place to be, there was so much more to life than the city had to offer and she wanted to explore. Armed with beauty and brains, Kalia was determined to leave the mediocre existence of the home life that her parents had carved out for themselves and their children, behind. Although her father was a successful attorney and her mother a teacher, her parent's chose to live a comfortable, yet ordinary life. She and her siblings never wanted for anything and they dressed well but not on the level that Kalia desired.

Since she was eight years old, Kalia was in love with Vogue magazine and haute couture. She was also a certified snob. No one knew how she got that way, she was simply, different. By the time she was in the fifth grade she coveted designer labels that she saw the rich girls in Buckhead wearing every time she visited Phipps Plaza and Lenox Mall. Even as young as she was, Kalia was sampling expensive wines, Champagne, foie gras and Caviar, which the parents of her rich friends served at their dinner parties. The Hudson's however, never even had fish in their home or any liquor to speak of. She didn't know why but her mother hated both things to the core. To keep up with those same friends, Kalia began shoplifting from some of the best stores and boutiques in Atlanta. Not only did she act like money, she looked like it as well. She knew better than to ask her parents for those kinds of clothes because they didn't believe in putting on airs.

"We live a good life, Kalia Rae," her dad would always say. "There's no need for us to try to keep up with the Joneses."

No one understood that Kalia never wanted to keep up with the Joneses. She wanted to *be* the Joneses.

"If you say so Daddy. But why do we always have to shop at cheap stores like, Dillard's and buy store brands at the grocery store? How embarrassing. We're one step away from getting food stamps," she pouted.

"Dillard's is a fine store young lady and you'd do well to remember that. Also, if you don't like the food that your mother and I provide for you, you are more than welcome to get a job and buy your own." It was the same old argument that no one ever won.

She wanted to be like the girl's in her school who were born with prestige and pedigree. The girl's whose parents were amongst the Who's Who of Atlanta's elite. Her parents could have been on that level if they were not so hell bent on being basic. For that, Kalia begrudged her parents and couldn't wait to leave the nest as soon as she could. How anyone could be happy living such a lowly lifestyle was beyond her. Even her siblings, who were as smart and beautiful as Kalia deemed herself to be, was happy with their lot in life.

As the youngest of five children, Kalia grew up resenting her siblings for their natural abilities and talents. Each of them had something unique about them that their parents praised. Except her. Kalia felt like she had to work three times harder than they did to compete with them. It was a self-imposed competition that only she was aware of. To outdo them, she had used her intelligence to get accepted into a top Atlanta private school. She felt she deserved better than a public-school education.

Her oldest sister, Kayla, was head of every school organization and team and served as class president in each grade until she graduated from Tri-Cities High School in East Point, Georgia where they lived.

But Kalia thought Kayla was stupid because she chose to attend Howard University instead of a 'good' school like Harvard. Kayla had been accepted at *every* university that she applied to, including Harvard, yet she chose a subpar HBCU. At least that's how Kalia felt. Not that Howard was a bad school; it simply wasn't on Kalia's level. She wanted to be better and have better than most people. And regardless of their race, Kalia thought she was too good for *everyone*.

Her brother Kyle Jr., or KJ, as he was affectionately known, was a basketball phenomenon and was slated to head to the NBA straight after high school. He was going to be a millionaire before he was twenty-one. Academics and athletics were his top priority, leaving him very little time to bother with his youngest sibling. They had a cool relationship but he was clueless as to who his little sister really was. So was her third oldest sibling, Kelli, who was older than Kennedi by six minutes.

Kelli had been accepted at the Tri-Cities School of Performing Arts because she had a voice that was blessed by

God Himself. She could sing anyone under the bus and her vocals had caught the attention of hot, young Atlanta producers, Jermaine Dupri, who was bursting on the scene with hits, as well as Kenny "Babyface" Edmonds and L.A. Reid of LaFace Records. It wouldn't be long before the world knew who Kelli Hudson was. Lastly, there was Kennedi, Kelli's fraternal twin, who could do it all but had no interest in anything except reading and writing. She was the most astute of all the Hudson clan and was the only one who had time enough to pay attention to all the misdeeds that Kalia did. Kennedi was a thorn in Kalia's side and she hated everything about her older sister. It was Kennedi who Kalia longed to get away from the most.

"I see you've been stealing again," Kennedi said when Kalia came in the house with a powder pink cashmere Chanel sweater.

"I haven't stolen anything, nosey. My friend Stacey Berkowitz bought this for me for my birthday," Kalia lied.

"Mmm, hmm. Sure, she did. It's interesting that all your wealthy friends are always buying you things. I wonder what Mother would learn if she called their parents to thank them for being so generous to you. I'm sure it would be quite interesting."

"Mind your business, Kennedi. You really need to get yourself a life and stay out of mine. It is so unbecoming that you are jealous of me, a mere child."

"Trust when I say that no one is jealous of you, Kalia Rae. If anything, I pity you. You have no clue about what's important and you're so out of touch with reality. I feel sorry for the unlucky bastard who has the misfortune of marrying your trifling, wanna-be, ass," Kennedi said softly before leaving Kalia with her mouth hanging open.

"One day, I'll show that bitch who is boss. Wait and see," she mumbled to the closed door.

A few weeks later, Kalia got her chance. Kennedi's boyfriend Justin came over to visit her sister who hadn't made it home from her part-time job yet. Kalia told him he could wait for her in the family room. He and Kalia were alone.

"So, what's up brother-in-law?" Kalia asked, swatting him on his thigh playfully.

"Nothing much. Just been chilling, hooping and things."

Justin Wade was the star basketball player at school and was being looked at by recruiters from the country's best universities.

"Right on. I saw your picture in the paper. You be doing your thing. I'm proud of you, dude." Kalia eased closer to him. "So, uh, you screwing my big sister or what?"

Unfazed by her forwardness, the young baller leaned back on the sofa and licked his lips.

"Nah. Kennedi is a good girl. All me and her do is kiss. She the wifey type, but I have some hoes who let me fuck so I won't get blue ball."

"Is that right?"

"Yep. What your little fine ass been doing? I know you be letting those young cats finger that tight little pussy of yours."

"Nope. This pussy too good for little ass boys. I need a real man. Someone like you," she said edging closer to her sister's boyfriend. "Damn, I think my box is juicing. You want to touch it for me and see, Justin?" She asked, raising the hem of her mini skirt.

"Hell yeah," he salivated, sliding his shaking fingers inside the young girl's snatch. "Damn, Kalia, your shit is hot and tight."

23

"Slide them in deeper, baby. You won't hurt me. I love the way your fingers feel inside me."

The teen used his index finger to fuck the young girl who writhed in pleasure on the leather sofa.

"Put two fingers in me baby. I want to come. I feel like I'm about to explode."

He obliged and added his middle finger to the sticky playground he played in. Kennedi would never let him do her like this and honestly, he didn't want to. He loved her and felt like she was the kind of girl a man married, not trifled with like some fling. But Kalia was different. She had slut written all over her. It would be easy to fuck her the way she sashayed her ass in front of him each time he visited. He figured it was a matter of time before she made her intentions plain. That time was now.

"Ooh, yeah baby, I'm coming. Finger me harder, boy I'm coming. I'm cu-mm-iii-nn-gggg," Kalia sang out.

Spent, she leaned back on the sofa and smiled in satisfaction.

"Not so fast. What you gon' do about this?" He said, pointing to the hard-on bulging in his Tommy Hilfiger Jeans. "My girl can't come home and see this shit."

"What you want me to do about it?" Kalia asked with an attitude. "I'm not letting you stick that thing in me. I am not ready for that."

"Bitch I ain't trying to fuck your young ass but you will take care of my dick like I took care of your hot ass pussy. Get your ass over here and get on your knees." He commanded. Justin unzipped his pants and pulled his dick out through the slit in his boxer shorts. "Come suck this shit, Kalia."

"What? I've never done that before," she said truthfully.

"First time for everything isn't it?" He asked sarcastically.

With Kalia positioned on her knees in front of him, he grabbed her head and shoved his dick in her mouth.

"That's right, slob on this dick bitch and get it wet. That's it. Ah, shit."

Kalia gagged at first but imagined the sweaty piece of meat to be a lollipop and she sucked and licked on it like it was such.

"Damn, Lia, your ass is a natural at this. Take this shit down your throat," he said, thrusting his hips up off the sofa.

The more he thrust, the harder she sucked. Kalia made sure his dick was wet and started massaging his balls with her small hands. Her head bobbed up and down as she got more involved in pleasing the young man. He was about to nut because his legs began to tense up. She learned about that from watching porn videos. His moans were getting louder and Kalia was glad that they were home alone. Or so she thought.

Too tired to knock on the door because Kalia's lazy ass wouldn't get up to let her in anyway, Kennedi took the time to dig her house key out of the bottom of her purse. The large entry way door closed as quietly as it opened. Setting her purse down on the table in the foyer, Kennedi removed her shoes as was custom in their home and walked down the long, carpeted hallway towards the family room. She was stunned to see her boyfriend of six months fingering her little sister.

"Whorish, bitch," Kennedi fumed. "I got something for her ass, though."

Kennedi walked quickly but quietly to her father's study and opened his file cabinet drawer.

"Please be charged. Please be charged," she pleaded. Kennedi pressed the power button on the small camcorder and was happy when the red light illuminated.

Hurriedly, she went back to the family room and stood behind the large tree plant and taped her little sister giving a blow job to her man. The camera lens was zoomed in to capture every facial expression that her conniving sister and unfaithful boyfriend made.

Kennedi gritted her teeth so hard her jaw ached. She was angry. But not at her man, only at her sister. She wasn't giving up her goods to anybody before marriage and that included him. She knew that he was fucking loose girls who had no morals. Clearly her sister was one of them. It didn't surprise her though. Kennedi had witnessed Kalia masturbating on several occasions but Kalia didn't know it. She would be mortified if she did. She was also privy to the fact that Kalia read erotica and secretly wished to have tons of sex according to the journal she kept that Kennedi, sneaked and read. Yes, her sister was a whore.

"Damn, I'm about to shoot this load," Kennedi heard her boyfriend yell. "Don't...stop...now."

Holding her head in place when she tried to pull back, he felt the first droplets of come pass the tip of his hard dick. As the volcano erupted, he forced her to swallow his sperm whether she liked the taste of it or not. Bucking his hips wildly, the long, thick dick was shoved down the young lady's throat, causing her to gag and her eyes to tear up.

"Shit. Swallow my babies, bitch."

One final thrust and hot semen filled her mouth. She swallowed some and spit out the rest. Kalia wiped her mouth and sat back on her haunches, smiling at a job well done.

"You sure you never sucked dick before, Lia? Your ass was way too good to be a beginner." his brow lifted inquisitively.

"I'm positive. I don't know why but pleasing you came naturally."

"*Cause you're a whore that's why,*" Kennedi whispered behind the tree.

"Girl, your ass is a certified head doctor. You good at listening to people and sucking dick. This should be a career for you," he said jokingly, but Kalia was seriously pondering his words. "Shit, I mean if a man ain't careful, he could easily get sprung off your young ass pussy and be willing to come out of pocket to keep a tenderoni like you happy and all to himself."

"Is that right? So, you want me to be all yours, is that it?" Smiling, Kalia thought about how devastated Kennedi would be if she took her boyfriend away.

Justin burst out laughing before responding. "Do I want you to be all mine? Hell naw. I love Kennedi. Your sister is the truth. Plus, I know if I can finger you after only talking to you for a few minutes, so can any other cat. Nah, I'm happy where I am."

Kennedi smiled at the exchange and continued recording.

"Well if you love my sister so much then why would you betray her by fingering me and making me suck your dick?" Hot tears threatened to spill over her eyelids as she spoke.

"Man, it ain't that much 'making' in the world. You make it seem like I raped you or some shit. Hell, you the one who came on to me. You came in here with that short ass skirt on, no panties and shit and opened your legs to me. Shit, if you put pussy on the menu a young buck like me is most definitely gonna order it. Especially if it's free."

"Fuck you Jay. I hate your ass," Kalia yelled as she ran up the back staircase towards her room.

Kennedi stopped taping and powered the camera off, removed the tape, placed it in her pocket and returned the camera where she got it. Later, she would put it up for safe keeping. Her boyfriend was coming out of the downstairs powder room when she entered the family room.

Nonchalantly she asked, "How long you been here, Jussy?"

"Almost an hour, I think. Your sister kept me company, though."

"I'm sure she did," she said, giving him the side eye.

"You ready to study? We have that big test Monday," he suggested.

"Sure, let's get busy."

Upstairs, Kalia stewed. She wanted to hurt her sister and make her out to be the laughing stock of the community when people found out that she lost her man to her younger sister. Turns out the joke was on her. Embarrassment coursed through her body as she thought about how brazen she had acted a few moments ago.

"I'll be damned if I fuck anyone anymore and not get shit out of it but a wet pussy. I see why some women sell it.

An hour later, Kalia's family had come home and before long, her mom was calling her downstairs for dinner. They were having fried chicken, green beans, dinner rolls and mashed potatoes with gravy. White gravy. Kalia's stomach churned ever so slightly when she put a fork full in her mouth. The gravy's creamy texture was reminiscent of the sperm that she gulped down earlier, although the gravy tasted much better.

"Swallow your food, Kalia Rae," her father said sternly.

"Yeah, swallow it, Kalia," Justin, who had stayed for dinner, leaned over and whispered.

Obeying her father, Kalia swallowed the potato and gravy mixture and hurriedly finished her dinner.

"May I be excused, please, Sir? I have some studying to do if I plan on taking the early high school entrance exams next week."

"Sure. Clear your place."

It took everything in her not to cry at the table. Kalia would not be able to face Justin every day knowing how he shunned her after she sucked his dick. Being intimate with him caused feelings of love to stir within her. Delusional, Kalia believed he felt the same for her deep down inside; and even though he was madly in love with her sister, a part of him loved her, also. No matter what she had to do, Kalia was going to pass the test next week and win the scholarship to the boarding school in Virginia. It was time for her to get the hell out of dodge.

By the time the testing date arrived, Kalia felt like a genius. Counting on her remarkable memory to help her ace the test, the young girl took her time to answer each question clearly and concisely. She would not be denied. And she wasn't. Kalia passed each exam with an almost perfect score. A few weeks later, Kalia's application to Gateridge Preparatory Academy in Alexandria, Virginia was accepted. Because her parent's combined income was below $350,000 annually, Kalia qualified for a full scholarship.

"It's absurd that our income is considered low to those pompous asses," her father said, shaking his head in disbelief.

"I agree. Kalia, are you sure that this is the type of school you want to be associated with? It's highly likely that the young lady's will look down on you and treat you like an outcast if they were to discover your financial aid status."

"I'm not worried about them, Mom. I'm there to receive the best possible education I can get. The fact that I can get it for free is a bonus."

In truth, Kalia had thought about the ramifications of being labeled 'poor' but was already putting a plan in place where no one would ever find out. She would be fine maneuvering amongst her peers. Three months after finishing eighth grade, Kalia was settled in her new dorm room. She took time in her freshmen year to get acclimated to her new surroundings and find out who was whom among the school's elite. She also studied the faculty, male and female alike to see who could best help her succeed in the school. Gateridge was going to help Kalia use what she had to get what she wanted and before she was through, she was going to have it all.

HOT GIRL

The years had been good to Kalia. Gateridge Prep's Elite adored her more than Britney Spears and The Backstreet Boys who were quite popular at that time. Upon arrival, she had quickly assessed the students and staff. Her game plan was to act haughtier than any of the girls there and make them believe that she was more than she really was. Kalia barely spoke to her classmates and when invited to join certain popular girls for lunch, she declined, opting to sit by herself. This intrigued the young girls and made them want to know her even more.

No one knew of Kalia's financial aid status and they never would. She made sure of that her freshman year. During orientation, Kalia overheard a few of the girls talking about the school's head mistress and her sexual orientation.

"I heard she liked young pretty girls and that she could eat the shit out of some pussy," Kalia heard as she hid in a bathroom stall.

"Hmm, interesting. I know I wouldn't mind if she licked my clit. I haven't come in months," a wealthy Latina student, whose voice Kalia recognized, said to her friend.

"Your ass is so nasty. A straight freak."

"Whatever, Mami. A tongue is a tongue to me. It doesn't matter. As long as she doesn't expect me to reciprocate."

After the girls' walked out, Kalia made it a mission to find out if what they said was true. A few weeks after her arrival, Kalia went to the young head mistress, feigning distress.

"How can I help you today, Ms. Hudson?" She asked. "Have a seat."

"Honestly, I don't know if you can." Kalia turned away in shame as she sat down.

"Why don't you let me be the judge of that."

"Well, Ms. Lewis, I keep having these dreams and they are scary and confusing. I don't know what to do." Kalia hung her head and began to wring her hands in her lap.

"How so? Are these dreams nightmares?"

"They may as well be. In them I am... I mean, they are... Oh, I can't even say it."

"What is it, Kalia? You know you can talk to me about anything. That's what I'm here for. Come on; tell me what's bothering you."

"I'm scared to say. I don't want you to look at me differently."

"Trust me young lady, there's nothing you can tell me that will shock me," Ms. Lewis reassured her.

"May I lock the door? I don't want anyone to come in and hear what I am about to say."

"Sure. If that will make you feel better. Please hold all my calls," she instructed her secretary.

After Kalia bolted the door and sat down she began her lie. "Well, these past few days I have been having dreams about making love and when I wake up, my panties are wet from having an orga-..." her voice trailed off.

Ms. Lewis smiled. "These dreams are normal for a girl your age. It's natural that your interest in boys manifests itself in your dreams. That should neither scare nor confuse you. You're perfectly normal."

"I would feel normal if I was dreaming about boys but I'm not." Kalia looked up when she heard Ms. Lewis take in a sharp breath. *Gotcha.*

"You mean, you dream about...girls?"

"Yes, ma'am. I don't know why either."

"Oh my. This is, um...interesting."

"See, I knew I shouldn't have said anything. Now you're going to think something's wrong with me." Kalia jumped up from the chair dramatically and darted toward the door.

Ms. Lewis hurried after her.

"Kalia, no. Please. Don't leave. I understand. Believe me."

Standing nose to nose and breathing heavily, Kalia leaned in and kissed her head mistress square on the lips. The lady stepped back.

"This isn't appropriate, Kalia."

"I know Ms. Lewis, but it's you," Kalia began and then turned away.

"It's me, what Kalia?" She asked, turning the young girl back around to face her.

"It's you, who I've been dreaming about, Ms. Lewis. Please don't deny me this. My body aches for you. I need you."

Not waiting for a reply, Kalia eased her tongue in the head mistresses mouth and caressed her right breast. Slowly, she kissed her until she felt the older woman relax against her body. Smiling, Kalia unbuttoned her school uniform blouse and then her lover's, lifting her bra barely above her breasts in the process.

"You look better than in my dreams," she whispered.

She flicked her hot tongue over Ms. Lewis's hard nipple before taking it into her mouth. She walked the head mistress over to the chaise lounge that was in the corner of her office and sat her down without taking the nipple out of her mouth.

"Open your legs for me," Kalia said sternly. The woman obliged. Kalia was in control and she loved it.

Her hand slid between the older woman's legs and she felt the warmth in the seat of her panties before putting her hands inside to touch the welcoming flesh. Using her middle finger to slide into the moist center, Kalia twirled it around inside and then moved it back and forth.

"More," Ms. Lewis begged.

Happily, she obliged. Three of Kalia's fingers played around in the hot pussy until she decided to go in for the kill. While Ms. Lewis was writhing in pleasure on the lounge chair, her young paramour got down on her knees and began sniffing around her center.

"Let me take my panties off," the woman suggested.

"No. I like it like this."

Moving the panties to the side, Kalia flicked her tongue over Ms. Lewis's clit. This was her first time eating pussy. It was tangy but not tart. Ms. Lewis had a minty smell in her twat that drove Kalia mad. Hungrily, she devoured her pussy, licking, biting and sucking.

"This is what I do to you in my dreams. And this, too. Let me show you. Get on your knees."

With her knees on the floor and her upper body on the chaise, Ms. Lewis was in for quite a surprise. Kalia reached in her bag and got a crystal anal dildo. Lying on her back, Kalia positioned herself between her lover's legs and began sucking on her clit again.

"Ooh we. Oh, yes. Don't stop," Ms. Lewis urged.

The sound of slurping filled the otherwise quiet office. Pussy juice saturated Ms. Lewis's sugar walls and Kalia slid the dildo in her pussy to lubricate it.

"Relax. When you feel the dildo on your ass, push out as I push in. It'll feel better."

Once the dildo was nice and lubed, Kalia slid it in. Gently she worked it round and round, in and out, getting her lover used to it. It hurt Ms. Lewis but because they were in her office, she couldn't scream out in pain or moan in pleasure as she would have liked. Kalia applied pressure to the hardened nub as she sucked and increased the speed of the dildo inside her lover. She slid two fingers inside her pussy hole so that both holes were penetrated and the way Ms. Lewis's legs began to shake, Kalia recognized that she was on the verge of exploding. A few aggressive strokes of the dildo and gentle sucking pressure on the clit and Ms. Lewis squirted her juices in the young girl's mouth.

"That was amazing Ms. Lewis. You were everything I dreamt about and then some. Thank you so much for making my dreams come true."

"Oh my gosh. I can't believe that I allowed you to do this. I can't believe that I loved it so much. This can never-"

"Please don't say that," Kalia interrupted. "Don't say this can never happen again. I need you, Carla Renee."

Taken aback hearing the teen call her by her full name, the woman sat up.

"How do you know my name, Kalia. No student at this school knows that."

"That was true until I came. Well, you're the one who just came but I digress," Kalia laughed. "I know so much about you my beautiful pedophile. Your parent's name, address, even what church they attend. Imagine how they'd feel knowing you were fucking a teenager. And a girl at that."

"What do you want from me?" Ms. Lewis questioned nervously.

"Not much, really. I need you to update my file to say that my parents earn over a million dollars a year. No one can ever know I was admitted on a scholarship." The last word tasted bitter on Kalia's lips. Scholarship. Financial aid. Assistance. Those words left a bad taste in her mouth.

"Okay. Is that all? Consider it done." She was relieved. Carla Lewis had been in this predicament before. Young girls never wanted much. They were stupid. All of them.

"Oh, you may be done but I'm not. I also need a stipend. These rich bitches have money for everything and I need that, too. I'm not unreasonable. You don't have to spend much on me. Make sure I have some money to shop on occasion. And one more thing," Kalia smiled, lowering her eyes.

This one was neither dumb nor stupid. Carla Lewis recognized that look all too well. Kalia wanted more.

"What is it young lady?" The headmistress asked with disdain.

"I want to be able to get this pussy at least once a week. Next time, you get to feast on me though." Kalia kissed the woman and rubbed her hand over her breasts once more before exiting the office. She was off to a very good start.

Once her records were altered, Kalia felt more self-assured about being at the exclusive school. During her freshman and sophomore years, Kalia made sure that she only hung with the crème de la crème of Gateridge Prep. Now at the close of her junior year, she considered herself to be the HBIC, head bitch in charge.

Grudgingly, she packed her bags at the end of the school year and prepared to begin her summer vacation at home. She would have preferred to travel the French Riviera or visit the ancient ruins in Greece like a few of her wealthy class mates. Instead, she was returning to a humdrum existence where she would be forced to interact with people she loathed...her family. During the summer, she was going to make sure to nurture those important connections while she was at home to keep her place as head of the class.

One day at home, she sat on the window seat in her room and smiled at her accomplishments. She got accepted into two prestigious schools, entered high school earlier than most and was being taken care of by one of the hottest women she knew. Kalia believed that she was hands down the Hudson's craftiest child. She was also the Hudson's only snobby child. Turning her nose up in distaste, Kalia looked around her room and snarled.

"When I have kids, they will not live in a dilapidated shack in a less than stellar neighborhood, nor will they have to share rooms. Ugh," she said out loud.

She got up and went over to her suit case and began to unpack the few things she dared to bring home. Thankfully, those returning to Gateridge kept the same rooms so she left most of her things there. Her parents would surely question where she got such high ticketed items like her Fendi winter coat, Chanel blouses and pant suits and Versace dresses.

Kalia didn't think anyone in her family could even pronounce the late designers name. Probably the only reason they had heard of him was because his murder made headlines. No, her family wasn't interested in designers or haute couture. They were satisfied shopping at cheap stores like The Gap and Macy's.

God I hope this summer passes quickly.

As Kalia was about to pull more clothes out of her luggage, the door to her shared bedroom burst open and her sister walked in.

"Well, if it isn't the Little Princess. Came back to grace us with your presence, huh? To what do we owe this displeasure?" Kennedi asked.

Kalia closed the lid on her suitcase. "I had to come home, Kennedi. Trust me, if I could be anywhere else in the world, I would."

"Hmm, I bet you would." Kennedi leaned over to look at the suitcase. "So, what nice stolen things do you have in there?"

"There's nothing in here stolen and you need to mind your fucking business. You're the main reason that I didn't want to come back to this hell hole."

"This *hell hole*, is your home Kalia. One day your butt is going to write a check your ass can't cash and then end up like Dorothy."

"Dorothy? Who's that?"

"That chick from Wizard of Oz who wished she was home."

"I swear you are so lame, Kennedi. Can you please give me some privacy? I was about to call one of my class mates."

"Yeah. Sure. I'll give you some privacy. I don't want to hear all those tales you're about to spew. Lying ass."

"Whatever."

After Kennedi left out, Kalia quickly put her things away before anyone else walked in. One of the problems of being the youngest was that her older siblings rarely showed her any respect. It didn't matter though. It was only a matter of time before she graduated from high school and started college. Once she did, she vowed that she would never return to that house again to live.

The days didn't pass as quickly as Kalia would have hoped. Each day she woke up she was forced to do one chore after another. It was stupid that her parents treated her like she was basic. It was fine that her other siblings did chores. They lived there in that house and should take care of it. She, on the other hand, was just visiting and felt that she should make her discontentment known.

"Mother, I am sure that you and Father are aware that I am only here for a few weeks at a time," she began.

"And? What's your point?"

"Well, I don't feel as if I should be subjected to doing menial chores like the others. I'm visiting. You don't make visitors do chores. That's rude."

"What's rude little girl is how you're standing over there thinking that you're better than your sisters and brother when you're not. You are as much a part of this family as everyone else and whether you're here one day or one month, you will do exactly what you're told, when you're told."

Don't remind me she said in her head. "Ugh," she sighed loudly. "Regardless of what you have us doing, there's no help for this place. We need to move into a better house in a better neighborhood and get out of the SWATs."

"This *place* as you refer to it is our home. You make it sound like a dump. I don't know what's gotten hold of you but I don't like it. I should have known sending you off to that school was a mistake. You're worse now than you ever were."

"Oh, don't blame the school, Mother. You're mad because I have the audacity to desire more than a remedial life like the one you have with Father. The two of you disgust me."

"Ooh Jesus, be a fence around this child. Girl if you don't get out of my face I promise you I will knock you so far East you'll end up in Decatur. And you better get your act together or else you will be attending Tri-Cities when school starts back. We disgust you? Leave then." her mother yelled.

Kayla ran into the kitchen where her mother was to find out what was going on.

"You okay, Ma?" She asked, looking from her mom to her baby sister.

"I'm fine. Your sister pissed me off that's all. Get out of my sight little girl. I mean it. Go, before you wish you had."

Kalia turned on her heels and ran out of the room.

"Mom, I've never seen you like this. What happened?"

"It's not important," she said and returned to cutting vegetables.

"I'll tell you what happened, Sis."

Kayla turned around to see her brother KJ standing in the door way.

"Your boujee ass sister told Mama that she was too good to do chores and that Mama and Dad disgusted her."

"Are you serious? And she's still standing? Did she really say that, Ma?"

"Yes baby, she did. But I'm not worried about her. She's just acting out."

"Acting out? She's showing her ass that's what she's doing. I can't believe you allowed her to speak to you that way. I'm gonna check her ass. She can't talk to you that way."

"Watch your mouth, Kayla."

"Watch my mouth? You let that little heathen disrespect you and you're telling me to watch my mouth?"

"Hey calm down, Sis. You're right, Mama. Kay is upset that's all. You know how we feel about you. We don't want anybody disrespecting you. No matter who it is," he added. "Come on Kayla, let's go to the mall and clear our heads."

When her kids left the kitchen, Karen set the knife down and stared out the window. Kalia had been a problem child ever since she was little and only got worse as years progressed. Karen thought that it was a phase that the girl went through but soon learned it was not. It was as if the teen hated her family. As much as Karen wanted to deny it, that was the truth.

Outside, Kayla and KJ met up with the twins and told them what went down in the kitchen. Since Kalia had been home, she had managed to do something to piss off everyone in the house. None of them wanted her there.

"God, I can't wait 'til summer is over and her ass is gone," Kellie said.

"You ain't never lied," KJ said. "Me and Kayla were about to go to the mall. Y'all want to roll?"

"Yep."

"You know it."

The group piled in the car and was about to back out of the driveway when Kalia ran out and stopped them.

"Where are you all going?"

"To hell if we don't pray," her brother. answered. "The mall. Why?"

"I want to go. Scoot over, Kelli," she said, reaching for the door handle.

"Nah, you good. We wouldn't want to subject you to riding in a hooptie. The Rolls Royce is in the shop getting detailed right now, "he joked. The siblings laughed.

"Yeah, we common folks would hate to tarnish your image. What would your Gateridge chums think if they saw you with us? Why, you could be ostracized," Kennedi added.

Kalia stepped back from the car as her brother backed up and watched them ride away.

For the rest of the Summer they excluded her from every activity that they did together and rarely spoke to her at the dinner table. They were angry with her. Even her mother had very little to say. Kalia could tell by the look in her mother's eyes that she had hurt her feelings. As much as she wanted to apologize though, she didn't. Her father was working so much she barely had a chance to see him and when she did, all he talked about were sports and politics. Neither of which Kalia was interested in.

Kalia happily returned to Gateridge and prayed that she didn't have to go home for a long time. When Thanksgiving and Christmas break came up, she was invited to Richmond to spend the holidays with her friend Rachel, whose parents owned new car dealerships up and down the Eastern seaboard. Her mother was usually the one who insisted she come home but since that day in the kitchen, it was as if her mother didn't care what her youngest did anymore. No one at home seemed to care. The following summer the Hudson's had given Kalia permission to accept a fellowship in London. Every chance she got to stay away from home she took. She didn't care whether she saw her family or not and they shared the sentiment. They didn't see Kalia again until she graduated high school.

THE FRESHMAN FIFTEEN

For most people, the freshman fifteen referred to the amount of weight that a person gained during their first year of college. For Kalia it meant the number of people she had already had sex with. Easily one of the most beautiful women on The Duke University campus, Kalia had made her way through many wealthy suitors. Men and women. None of them had a problem exchanging great sex for the designer labels and money she coveted. To protect herself and keep her name from being sullied, Kalia made sure that she had some dirt on each of her lovers so that they wouldn't run around campus, spreading her business and slut shaming her.

Her last boyfriend, Brett Matthews, was by far the richest and cutest guy she had been with. And for a white dude, he was well hung. One thing that she loved about Brett was that his family was one of the most notable families in the Carolina's and they liked black people. She could have seen herself as Brett's wife. Unfortunately, he didn't. The night that they broke up she found out why.

"Oh yes, Brett. Fuck my ass, baby. That's it."

Brett pounded her backside, skin slapping skin, until he climaxed inside her.

"Where do you see us in five years, babe?" Kalia asked him, running her fingers down his chest, after a bout of mind-blowing sex.

"Well, seeing as how this is my last year in school, I see me running my father's London office, engaged to the most beautiful woman I know, planning the biggest wedding that North Carolina has ever seen."

"Really, babe?" Kalia sat up excitedly. "I was thinking the same thing. Well, minus the whole living in London part, but everything else is spot on. I can't wait to be your wife."

Laughing as he sat up, Brett corrected her. "Bitch, I know you don't think that I'm talking about you do you? Please, there's no way I would marry someone like you. My family would disown me."

"What are you talking about, Brett? Your family loves me, they like black people and furthermore, I am not a bitch."

"You don't get it, do you? Your skin color doesn't matter, Kalia. It's your morals and standards that they'd have a problem with."

"What are you talking about my morals and standards? There's not a classier woman on this campus and you and I both know that."

"Nah, there's not a *trashier* woman on this campus and you and I both know that. I know all about the blackmail and shit. Matter-of-fact, lemme show you something."

Brett hopped out of bed and grabbed his laptop off his desk. He plopped down on the bed and navigated through some files before clicking on the one he was looking for. He turned the volume up.

"Watch."

As the picture became clear, Kalia was stunned at what was playing on the screen. It was her in an empty classroom with the audio-visual instructor, Mr. Warrington. She was sitting on his desk with her legs crossed in a hot pink mini skirt. Although the incident happened months prior when school first began, she remembered it like it was yesterday. Horrified, she watched the screen as she uncrossed her legs and spoke.

"Mr. Warrington, this is what you do to me, "she had said, placing his hand between her warm thighs. "Don't you want to taste me baby?"

Brazenly, Kalia dipped her fingers into her wetness and put the tangy nectar on her teacher's lips. He licked them hungrily and succumbed to the temptation. Without delay, he rolled his desk chair directly in front of Kalia, threw her legs over his shoulders and dived in her pussy, head first. Even through the computer's speakers, it was clear, how wet she was and how noisily he ate her pussy. She tried to turn away but Brett grabbed her head and pointed it towards the screen.

"Don't get shy on me now. The best part is coming up."

Brett held her head forcefully in place and laughed as the soft porn video continued.

"This is my favorite part right here. Look at your eyes," he laughed. "Them shits are rolling in the back of your head. I know your ass was getting ready to bust right here 'cause that's the way you look when you're coming for me."

Sure enough, Kalia was about to come. Hell, Mr. Warrington had made her climax like no other man had. Thinking about how good his tongue felt on her hard clit made her wet. The camera was right above her and caught her facial expressions so well. Her eyes closed and her jaws clenched in the final throws of her orgasm. Moving quickly before he had a chance to gather his rational thoughts, Kalia unzipped Mr. Warrington's pants, freed his hard dick and jumped on it. She rode him while he sat in the chair like he was a mechanical bull.

"Yeah, that's that same shit you do with me, too. Your ass is a pro at this."

Kalia got up off the bed and tried to walk away. Brett slapped her ass and then grabbed her hand, pulling her back down on the bed.

"What is it, Brett? You've made your point."

Kalia fumed as the wheels in her head turned trying to figure out how he got that tape. Now it didn't matter if she had anything on him because he had something more damning on her. Of course, she was sure that people would be interested in what she had. She could always dumb her tape down. After all, students slept with teachers all the time. And both she and Mr. Warrington were two consenting adults.

"Not really," he said, closing the laptop. "I know what you're thinking, too. I got the tape out of the camcorder I had set up in Mr. Warrington's class. I was making a documentary on human behavior. It was supposed to be a side by side comparison on how we act when we know we're being watched versus when we think we're not. Teach, forgot that I had the camera in place. Imagine my surprise when I saw what I had captured. I got an A in the class thanks to you."

"You knew I had slept with him when you first asked me out?"

"Yes."

"Then, why did you?"

"Your reputation preceded you, Kalia. I know about the tapes and photos that you have of me and a few of my frat brothers' sexual proclivities. They all came to me begging for my help to get them back. Blackmail has been very lucrative for you on this campus. It used to be anyway. Your gravy train has come to a stop and this is where you get off."

"Wha- what do you mean?" Kalia fumbled.

"Well my nasty Nubian queen, I was paid to put an end to your lascivious shenanigans and my work here is done."

"Paid? By whom?" Kalia couldn't believe her ears.

"Sarah, Michael, Charles, Coach Dillon, Lou, Trip, Patrick, Megan and even Mr. Warrington threw some money in the pot."

"Say what you will but I still have my treasure chest full of goodies," she boasted, referring to the videotaped evidence and pictures she had on each person he mentioned.

"Uh, yeah. About that. You don't have that anymore. See, when you and I first started fucking, I knew you would film us. So, before you planted your camera, I planted mine. The day I took you to Belle's for dinner and treated you to the day spa, I had some techs come in your room and install a few hidden cameras. I was actually watching you from my room when you set up your camera for our little rendezvous."

"I don't believe you."

"You don't have to. Believe this though." Brett pulled a box from under his bed and it contained a small, portable safe. "Does this look familiar?" He asked revealing her 'treasure chest'.

Kalia dropped her head in defeat. Every video, every picture…everything was in that safe and Brett had it all.

"What do you want, Brett?"

"What *WE* want is for you to leave this school and never darken our doorways again. Take your scheming, conniving ass back to Atlanta. We don't want your kind here."

"Leave school? You must be outta your mind. I've worked too hard to get here to let anyone take it away from me. I don't have to leave school and you or no one else can make me."

Brett shook his head. "That's where you're wrong. I told my dad that you had a video of me in a compromising position and how you planned to leak the tape and he immediately went to work. His attorney is the brother of our dean of admissions and together they eighty-sixed your scholarship. You know the one that no one was supposed to know you were here on."

"I can't believe that you would do this. This is my education you're playing with. How can you be so callous?"

"If it ain't the pot calling the kettle black. Callous? You're the one who threatened to release the tape of you fucking Michael in the ass with a strap-on. What would that have done to him and his life? His basketball career? You didn't care about him. You don't care about me. All you care about is your damned self. You're like a black widow spider except you don't kill the body, your target is the soul. You lure people in with that soft voice and understanding and then once you have us where you want us, you go in for the kill. Your venom is your good pussy and great head."

"Hmm, I wonder what your father would think if I told him that you sucked that same strap-on like it was a baby's bottle."

"You'll never know, will you?" Brett feigned a yawn. "Alas, I tire of this meaningless banter. Be gone peasant. Your time to depart has come." He shooed her away with his hand.

Fuming, a tearful Kalia dressed and left. She really liked Brett and had planned their future together in her mind. Once she got back to her dorm all she could do was cry and mourn the loss of what could have been a wonderful, rich life for her. That was months ago. At the end of the term, she returned home. For good. Her family didn't ask why she left school and she didn't offer a reason.

Now Kalia sat in her bedroom, angry about having to attend a local university in the fall. Although Brett and his father orchestrated a transfer to Georgia Tech on the same scholarship she was on at Duke, Kalia was bitter and angry that she wasn't going to an Ivy League university.

Disappointed, Kalia began to cry. How could she end up back in this place with *these* people? She hated her family. She couldn't stand her mother and the only siblings she did like was Kayla and KJ. The relationship with her father was okay but Kalia felt like he was a punk. He went along with any and everything that her mother advised.

"Weak bastard," she mumbled through tears. Exhaling, she dried her face and began applying her makeup. If she had to be in Atlanta, she may as well make the best of it. At least she wasn't in a Podunk town with a bunch of hicks. In Atlanta, her beauty and brains would take her far. The more she thought about the possibilities, the more her outlook improved.

"Humph while I'm sitting up here mad because life gave me lemons, I need to make the best lemonade possible," she said to the mirror.

Kalia's best friends from Gateridge Prep, who were also from Atlanta and attended Georgia Tech wanted her to go to a new club in Buckhead and she agreed. If she was going to find herself a rich husband, she was going to have to go where the rich hung out. She took great pains in choosing the right outfit. To attract money, one had to look like money. Her cell phone rang and she looked at the caller I.D. It was one of her best friend's, Anika.

"Hey Boo. You excited about tonight?" Her friend asked.

"I guess. It kinda feels weird being home. I feel so outta place."

"Awe friend. It's gonna be okay. But hell, you're home and must make the best of it. We need to get us one of these fine ass ball players or rappers or some shit like that. I mean school is cool, but shit, it's time for me to be a kept woman."

"I know right. We got to get it."

The two friends talked a few minutes longer then ended the conversation to continue dressing. The door to her room burst open and in walked her twin sisters, Kelli and Kennedi, as she was about to put on her bra.

"Hey Kalia," Kelli said, hugging her sister who was standing, covering her boobs with her hands. "What's up?"

"Hey. What are you two doing here?"

"We live here, remember? It's us who should be asking you that anyway," Kennedi said frostily. "After all, aren't you the one who told me that you would never return to this dump again?"

"Trust me, Boo. This is very temporary."

"I don't understand you lil' sis," Kelli began. "We live in a nice home. Always have. Our parents worked hard for us to live well and yet you turn your nose up at them and us. All because you don't have a Buckhead address? What is wrong with you?"

"I'm perfectly fine. It's you all with the issues. If you feel that this is nice, then that's on you. I've seen how the other half lives and honey, its way better than this."

"My poor, foolish, little sister. I would feel sorry for you if I cared enough about you. You think because you went to a private school your whole life and managed to steal a few designer clothes that you're better than us, but you're not. The only difference between you and us is that you will more than likely have to suck your way to the top because that's the only thing you're good at."

"Kennedi, don't say that," Kelli gasped. Although she didn't agree with Kalia's views on anything, she was still her sister.

"Tsk, tsk, big Sis. Your ass is so fucking pathetic and I am bored with this conversation. So, if you two will excuse me, I need to finish dressing." Kalia began putting her lace, pushup bra on. She turned her back in dismissal hoping her sisters would get the point.

"Whatever. Arguing with your dumb ass, I almost forgot what I came up here to tell you. Justin, that bum you said I date, well, he just signed lucrative seventy-five million dollars, three-year deal to play with the Heat."

"Good for him. But that ain't got shit to do with you though," Kalia bit back frostily.

"Actually, it does. They are getting married, Kalia. Mom sent you an invitation. Didn't you get it?" Kelli finished her thought and Kennedi wiggled her fingers, showing off the huge rock she wore.

"I don't recall seeing it. If I can make it, I'll come. If not, I'm sure you understand. Congrats." Jealousy coursed through her veins like blood.

She may have received it but she never opened any mail from home. It all went to the trash can as soon as she saw who it was from. Had it been important they would have called instead of writing.

Kennedi and Kelli both shook their heads and then left the room. There was no getting through to their sister. She was on a different planet most times. Kalia breathed easier when they left. Justin had done very well for himself. Deep inside, she always believed that he would. He still haunted her dreams many nights even though what happened between them was so long ago. She had really liked him and genuinely hoped by messing with him he would leave her sister and get with her.

"I may need to pay Mr. Wade a visit and give him some of this good-good. I'm sure my prudish ass sister still ain't giving it up."

An hour later, Kalia and her friends, Anika and Riley were standing in line at Atlanta's hottest new club, Swerve. Anyone who was anybody was there. Kalia was dressed to impress and she was not about to stand in line all night.

"Ri-, I thought that you said you could get us in?" The agitation could be heard in Anika's voice.

"I know right," Kalia chimed in. "We look too good to be standing in line with these basic bitches."

A few girls who were within earshot gave Kalia and her friends funky looks and sucked their teeth. One of them looked like she wanted to hit Kalia in the face but didn't move.

"Damn. When have you guys known me to lie? If I said I could, I can. Shit we just got here." She dialed a number in her cell phone. "Hey love. We're outside. Yes. It's three of us. Okay, see ya in a sec."

"Who was that?" Both Kalia and Anika asked.

"My cousin Ronnie. He's part owner in this club. He told me yesterday he was going to set us up in the VIP section and make sure we have bottle service."

"Now that's what's up."

"Oh, I almost forgot," Riley started. "If either of you are interested in psychiatry, my dad's practice is offering an internship for two months in his new office."

"Are you serious?" Anika asked incredulously.

"As a heart attack."

"Did I miss something here? What's so great about doing a psych intern?" Kalia always thought Anika and Riley were daft, this confirmed it.

"Dr. Sutton's new office is in Lyon, Kalia."

"And? What's so special about that? Lyon, Georgia. I've never even heard of that small ass town."

"No bitch. Lyon, France. An hour away from Paris."

"Get the fuck outta here. Oh, hell yeah. I'm most definitely down with that."

"I'm not, but I'm down to travel and check out the new office," Anika added.

"I figured you would be, Kalia. We can tell my dad and then get the paperwork done immediately. We leave next week. Your passport is still valid, right?"

"You know it. Next week? O-m-gee, this couldn't have come at a better time. I was arguing with my sisters earlier about being stuck in that hell hole you call a house."

"Well that settles it. The Three Musketeers are going to take over Paris."

Riley's cousin, Ronnie Sutton, sent a bouncer out to escort the young ladies inside the club. As promised, they were set up VIP style with their own server who kept the bottles coming. All three of them were under 21 but no one asked and they didn't tell. Shortly after they entered the club, a few very handsome men were brought to the VIP area and were seated in the section across from Kalia and her girls. They all looked and walked like money.

One guy was sporting a diamond Presidential Rolex and wearing a pair of $1500 tennis shoes. Kalia could recognize Giuseppe Zanotti's a mile away. From head to toe she was checking him out and at the same time, he was checking her out, also.

"I'm going over there and introducing myself to that fine ass man who looks like Usher. I might make him want to leave the one he's with and start a new relationship tonight."

Anika and Kalia watched as Riley sashayed across the room and introduced herself to the guys. The well-dressed one, Kalia had her eyes on, stood so that Riley could sit down and he made his way over to where Kalia and Anika sat. He leaned down and lifted Kalia's right hand to his soft lips.

"Hello beautiful. I am Colby Byron, and I am going to rock your world."

A DATE WITH PRINCE CHARMING

Colby Byron was a man of his word. In a matter of days, he had managed to show Kalia a side of Atlanta that she had never seen before. From dining to shopping, even the clubs he took her to, was different. Even though she was born and raised there, it was all new to her. There are things that go on in the city that only the very rich and wealthy are privy too. And although Kalia managed to wear all the new designer labels and had rich friends, she had never experienced the things that Colby showed her. Most of the clothes she wore were either stolen or someone got them for her. She hadn't really experienced the luxury of shopping in the upscale stores.

Shortly after she met him, he took her to lunch at one of Atlanta's most exclusive bistro's called Crème'. It was almost impossible for a 'regular' person to get a reservation there. The waiting list for commoners was almost a year long. You had to be a part of Atlanta's upper echelon to get a seat.

"Welcome back Mr. C. This way please," the pretty hostess said. She seated the couple at a table near the window and that served to feed Kalia's ego more. It was everything to her that people could walk by and see her eating in a place they couldn't even open the door to.

"Did she call you Mr. C?"

"Yeah. It's an inside joke. It means Mr. Cash. She's always teasing me about having money," Colby answered.

"Oh. Wow, look at this menu. It's *something*," she said pursing her lips and scratching her head. She was referring to the prices. This was her first time seeing a bottle of water that cost seventeen dollars. *Where the hell did they get it? Heaven?* She thought inwardly.

"May I recommend the Eggs Benedict? It's one of the best dishes on the menu?" He suggested.

The Eggs Benedict Florentine was forty-five bucks. Kalia felt like a pauper. Usually when she went places, she paid no attention to the prices. Especially since someone else was footing the bill but this was different. These prices were so bold and in your face, she couldn't help but take notice. She liked Colby. His confidence was through the roof and he was so suave and elegant in all his mannerisms and he was generous to a fault. The way he gently held Kalia's elbow when she exited the car to the subtle way he guided her by placing his hand on the small of her back let her know he was in control and that turned her on.

"So, tell me about yourself," she flirted.

"Well, I'm an only child who's spoiled senseless and used to getting what he wants," Colby said with a bit of cockiness in his voice.

"Is that right? And what is it that you want, Colby Byron?"

"You."

"So far you're making a valiant effort. But um, tell me more about you. Do you work? Are you in school?"

"No, I don't work. My Mom never wanted me to. She said that would all come in due time but for now concentrate on my education. I'm studying for my degree in engineering at Georgia Tech this fall. I was at MIT but chose to come home to be closer to my mother."

"How old are you? Shouldn't you be working on an advanced degree by now old man?"

"I'm twenty-two," he stated. "Same age as you."

"I'm only nineteen old man. Well, almost anyway."

"Nineteen? How did you get in the club then?"

"Riley's cousin is part owner of the club. Is my age a problem?"

"Nah..you're perfect in every way."

They talked almost an hour over brunch and then Colby took her shopping at Phipps's Plaza. He lavished her with gifts and gave her the receipts in case she wanted to return things. It was a huge change from stealing.

"What do you want from me?" Kalia asked him. "All this," she said sweeping her hand over the bags, "this isn't the typical thing you do for a woman you recently met. Hell, I don't know too many husbands who do shit like this."

"You'll learn that I'm not the typical man. And don't use profanity around me. That's an ugly trait in a woman." Colby got a look in his eyes that let Kalia know not to challenge anything he said.

"Alright. But let's keep it real. What do you want from me? Some as-, I mean sex?"

"If that's all I wanted I could've gotten it the night we met. I'm trying to cultivate a relationship here. You got a problem with that?"

"No. Not at all. I want to get to know you better but I will be leaving for Paris in a few days and I'll be gone for two months. I got an internship there."

"That's hot. I'm very happy for you. And don't worry, two months is nothing. For what I have planned for you, I'd wait forever. I'm a very patient man."

"We'll see, Colby Byron. We shall see."

Kalia was on cloud nine.

Meanwhile, the atmosphere in the Hudson household was tense. Kalia's dad didn't understand how his daughter could accept an internship so far away and not discuss it with her parent's first. Karen was over it. If her daughter wanted to leave, she could.

"Kyle, I don't know why you're wasting your breath on this child. She's told us in no uncertain terms that she hates it here. Why bother?"

"Praise God, woman. You finally said something that I agree with," Kalia smarted off.

"You watch your mouth young lady and don't speak to your mother that way or else I'll…"

"Or else you'll what, Dad? I don't see the big deal here. It's not like you guys are gonna have to foot the bill. You can continue to save your pennies like you've been doing."

"Little girl, the Lord is going to strike you down for disrespecting us like this," her mom said, getting teary eyed.

"Yeah, yeah. Look, are you two finished? I still have a few things to pack and then I'm going out. Don't wait up."

Kalia stormed out of the room leaving her parents with their mouths wide open. She knew how far she could take it with Karen and Kyle. They were not like most black parents. If they were, her head would be in one room and her body in the other if she ever deigned to speak to them that way. But her parents were…pushovers.

Two hours later Kalia found herself spread eagle across a king-sized bed at the Hilton. She took her right index and middle fingers and parted her wet pussy lips.

"Don't you want to come play in my wetness?" She asked

"You know I do. But first, I would love to feel those big, juicy lips wrapped around this dick. Don't you want to suck on this hardness?"

"You know I do, baby. Come here."

Kalia slid to the edge of the bed and took his hard dick in her mouth. He threw his head back in pleasure. She licked around the head of the shaft and then spit on it to get it wet. Slowly she massaged his dick and sucked it hard, alternating between slurps and strokes. Her tongue traveled down the length of his shaft and settled on his balls. She licked between the sack like it was a pair of cherries and moaned in delight when he whispered her name.

With her free hand, she rubbed her hardened clit. It wasn't long before she could feel the heat in her toes travel up her legs. The faster she sucked him the quicker she stroked herself.

"I'm about to come baby," she moaned.

"Not like that," he said. "Turn over and get on the bed."

Reluctantly, Kalia stopped sucking his dick and assumed the doggy-style position on the end of the bed. She was face down, ass up.

"Stroke that pussy for me," he yelled.

"Yes, baby."

He fingered her pussy as she rubbed her clit and he used the juices from her hot box to lube his dick. His large hands spread her ass so he could get a better view of her pussy. The more she stroked it the creamier it got.

"This is it, baby. I'm about to come. Please put your dick in me," she begged.

"You got it."

He positioned his dick at the entrance.

"Wait. What? No!"

With one strong thrust, he shoved the entire length of his nine-inch dick in her asshole.

"Ahh." Kalia screamed out. "Please stop. It hurts so bad."

"Relax. It'll be over before you know. Ah, shit. You're so tight. This feels so good. I'm about to bust."

"Oh, please. I can't take it. Please take it out."

"Just. A. Few. More. Strokes. Ah, shit. I'm coming."

He pulled his dick out and spun Kalia around so fast she almost fell off the bed. Creamy nut shot in her face as he pulled her mouth towards his squirting dick.

"Suck this shit. Ah, yes. That's my girl. Fuck." He through his head back in pleasure as he released his seed.

Kalia gagged on the sour nut, swallowing some, spitting out most. Her body ached and it hurt to sit on her backside. This was her first time being fucked in the ass without lube or a warning of what was to come. Hot tears streamed down her face as she watched him hastily dress after he finished.

"I know it hurt this time but you'll get used to it. Get some lube and keep it in your purse. I want to take that ass again. That's what I like. Holla at'cha later Shawty."

The door closed before Kalia could form a sentence. Stunned, all she could do was crawl in the bed and wrap herself up in the comforter. At that very moment, she felt used and dirty like she did all those years ago. Played and betrayed. For as much as she wanted to see him, she never should have called and hooked up with Justin.

EDUCATING LIA

Kalia was enamored with Donald Sutton. He was the most handsome and debonair gentleman she had met to date. Additionally, he was the wealthiest and most sought-after psychiatrist on two continents. Riley was blessed to have a father like him. He was well traveled, well-spoken and spent money like it grew on trees. He believed in living life versus merely existing, unlike her parents. The more time she spent with the Sutton's the more she disliked her own dismal family. Thinking about them soured her mood and it showed on her face.

"Hey, young lady. Why the scowl on your face? You're sitting at one of the finest restaurants on the world-famous Avenue des *Champs-Élysées*. You should be happy," Dr. Sutton said.

"Yep. Especially, since you're enjoying all of this with your besties," Riley chimed in.

"Sorry, guys. I was thinking about my family. You know how my parents irk me."

Dr. Sutton winced. "Kalia, that's not the way to talk about your parents. They have done a remarkable job raising such a fine young woman. You should be grateful."

"I am," she lied. "It's only that we had a slight disagreement before I left and I was thinking about it."

At least that part was true. Kalia and her sister, Kellie had exchanged words about a text Kellie saw in Kalia's phone to her sister's fiancé. It was innocent, thank God, but Kellie thought that Kalia was up to no good. Their mother got involved in the tiff and that's when things really spiraled out of control.

"Kalia," their mother began. "You need to stop acting like you're too good for this family and straighten up and fly right. Whether you like it or not, you're a Hudson."

"Ugh, stop reminding me. If you're happy to be a part of such a mediocre existence, then that's fine. But don't drag me down to hell with you. I hate this family and I am tired of living like a pauper with you mutherfucker's. I swear I hate all you bitches."

After Kalia picked herself up off the floor she was seeing stars.

"I can't believe you hit me," she eyed her mother.

"She didn't. I did," Kelli said. "Since you hate it here so much then pack your shit and get on. Fuck you and feed you 'cause we don't need you."

"Bitch this isn't your house and you can't tell me what to do." She yelled angrily, lunging for her sister. She was stopped dead in her tracks.

"She can't. But I can," her father said, holding onto her shirt tail. "I've tolerated your insolence far too long. I thought if I gave you time and space that eventually you would grow out of this spoiled, poor little rich girl routine, but no, you've gotten worse. Pack your bags and get them out of this house. When you come back from Paris, you can't come here. These 'mutherfucker's and 'bitches' think that you can kiss all of our asses collectively."

Kelli smile with pride.

"But, Daddy, I don't have anywhere to go," Kalia cried.

"Should've thought of that. I told you that you only had one more time to disrespect my wife. Well that time has come. Be safe out there little girl and pray. You're gonna need God on your side."

The sound of a fork clanging on the plate brought Kalia back to the present.

"Well I'm sure it wasn't that bad," Dr. Sutton said. "I think you youngsters need to realize that parents aren't perfect. We make mistakes, too."

"It is that bad, Dr. Sutton. My father kicked me out the house because he didn't approve of the guy he *thought* I was dating. He didn't even allow me to explain that I had just met the guy. I don't know what I'm going to do," she lied skillfully.

"Aren't you staying in the dorms when we go home?" Anika asked, believing all that she heard.

"Yes. I'm thinking about holidays. Where will I go?" She said softly.

"Don't you worry about that, little lady. By the time Thanksgiving rolls around, I'm sure you all will have mended your fences. If not, you are always welcome to join us. Now let's eat this wonderful repast and do some shopping, shall we?"

The next day, Kalia was filing some charts in Dr. Sutton's office. The more she watched him work the more she thought about exploring psychiatry as a profession. She had spied his client list and learned that he had some world-famous clients on his roster. Everyone who was anyone came to him for one thing or the other. She wanted to be like him. Rich and famous.

"Kalia, can you come in here a moment? Close the door behind you. Have a seat."

"Yes, Sir?" She asked.

"I wanted to talk to you about things back in Atlanta. Are you sure that you're okay? I saw the sadness on your face yesterday at lunch and it concerned me. I didn't want to bring it up in front of the girls because it's your private affair." Dr. Sutton got up from his desk and sat on the sofa next to Kalia.

"Thank you, Dr. Sutton. I know most young adults say this but I don't think my parents understand me at all. They think that I have a demon inside me all because I want to live better than I was raised and have nice things. Is that so wrong?"

"Not at all. You're a very beautiful woman. You deserve the best. Why not go for it?"

Dr. Sutton's voice changed in that moment. It got lower. Sexier. A bit seductive. Kalia noticed the bulge in his pants growing as well.

"Indeed. Why not go for it?"

Kalia stood up, licked her lips while keeping her eyes on his crotch and began unbuttoning her shirt and unsnapping her bra that hooked in the front.

"Got milk, Kalia?" He asked, pulling her onto his lap.

"Mmm, Dr. Sutton. That feels so good."

Slowly, he lavished her nipple gently sucking and biting until it was hard. Then he pulled her other nipple in his hot mouth and made love to it. Smoothly he pulled the panties down from under her short skirt and slid two fingers inside her wet, inviting pussy. He circled them around and then pulled them out, licking the creamy nectar from his fingers.

"Juicy. That's how I like it. Take the skirt off and get on your knees."

Kalia turned on the sofa, got on her knees and tooted her ass in the air. Dr. Sutton eased his condom covered dick into the hot pocket and exhaled.

"Ah, shit. Arch that back for me baby and take all this dick."

Kalia bounced her ass cheeks, showing off her skills and he slapped them hard, turning her on by his unnecessary roughness. He gripped her hips and pounded her pussy, watching her cream his dick. For an older man, he was hung. His girth surprised Kalia but she took all eight inches of the thick dick.

"Oh yea, big daddy. Beat this pussy up while I play with my clit, baby. Make me come Big poppa."

"I love it when you call me Big Poppa. Turn on your back. I want to see you rub that kitty. I want to see your face when I make you come."

Once Kalia got on her back, Dr. Sutton spread her legs like butterfly wings. Before he slid his dick inside he leaned over and licked her stiff clit. He made lazy circles around the nub and sucked on it until her legs began to quake. Kalia licked her lips as he pleasured her.

"Oh, that little girl is getting ready to come, isn't she? I know the signs well." He sucked on her clit and fingered her pussy and her legs began to shake violently. "I want to come inside you," he said, removing his rubber.

"Do what you want, Daddy. This pussy is all yours."

Kalia fingered her pussy with three fingers and rubbed her clit. Dr. Sutton impaled his dick in her tight asshole, stretching her out to accommodate his size.

"Uhn. Oh. Yes." Her face contorted in pleasure.

"Look at that cream. It tastes as good as it looks. Magnificent."

The creamier she got the harder he pumped, the faster she rubbed. They were both getting ready to come.

"Hey, Lorna. Is my dad in his office?" They both heard Riley ask.

"Yes, Dear. He was on a conference call earlier but you can go on in. Be quiet when you walk in, he may still be on the call."

Dr. Sutton saw the door knob turn ever so slightly. He panicked but was too close to coming to pull out. If his daughter caught him, he would blame the seduction on her whorish friend. The knob stopped twisting when Riley's cell phone rang.

"Tell Daddy, I'll be right back. I need to take this call in private."

Saved by the bell. Literally. Every nerve ending in Kalia's body was charged. No matter where Dr. Sutton touched her it felt as if she was touching a television with a wet hand.

"Oh, Daddy. I'm about to come. Come with me baby. Come in my ass, now."

Dr. Sutton growled and threw his head back as his hot seed spilled inside her. He sounded like a wounded animal in the woods.

"That was amazing," he said. "We will do that again, my dear." That was a promise.

The two of them dressed in record time and Dr. Sutton had Kalia spray the room with odor neutralizer to rid the room of the smell of sex. As soon as Kalia put the can in the drawer the door opened and Riley glided in.

"Hey guys. What'cha doing?"

"Hey darling. I was teaching Kalia how to take, uh dictation."

Kalia smiled and looked near the sofa. Her panties were peeking out of the cushion. Fuck. Riley was about to sit right next to them.

"Riley, you haven't seen your dad, all day. Give this man a hug." Kalia made a mad dash to the sofa and scooped her panties up, shoving them in her skirt pocket.

This was going to be a very interesting internship.

HEAD OF THE CLASS

Make what you do so original and coveted, people have no choice but to come to you to receive that service. If you do that, I guarantee you will never be broke again.

Kalia lay across Dr. Sutton's chest, stroking it gently; replaying the words he told her not fifteen minutes prior. She had come to enjoy the talks they would have after good loving. The doctor was so intelligent and caring. He offered her good advice on everything concerning life and love. Tonight, he was merely getting to know her. Asking her questions about her goals and future, showing a genuine interest in the young woman.

"Tell me what your interests are…who you be with…how to make you smile…what numbers to dial."

"Okay, Biggie. You really liked him, huh? That's the only rapper I've ever heard you quote."

"Yes. I loved his style. He was a kind young man. I had the pleasure of meeting him shortly before his passing. Hip-hop suffered a great loss when he died. Pac too. Those two artists brought such originality to the industry. It can't be duplicated."

"Wow. I had no idea you liked rap so much. You never cease to amaze me, Doctor."

"We can forego the formality of you calling me doctor, don't you think? I mean, we do know one another a little better now. I'm like any other man, how do I amaze you?"

"I love calling you that. I like playing "doctor" with you and you amaze me because you are so down to Earth. You have a million degrees, wealthy beyond my comprehension, have hobnobbed with everyone from President and First Lady

Obama to Queen Elizabeth. You are so well-spoken you could be an English teacher, yet you love hip-hop and hot wings and you live only a few miles from where you grew up in the SWATS. Anybody else would have moved to Buckhead or Sandy Springs."

"I love Southwest Atlanta or the SWATS as we love to call them. That's home for me. There's nothing wrong with either of the places you mentioned but I can live as well on the south side as I can up north and save money to boot. My home appraises at two million dollars but I only paid a half a mil for it. The problem with some black people is that when we get money we are quick to get out of the hood instead of trying to build it up."

"I wouldn't exactly call your neighborhood the 'hood', would you? You live in a gated community with a security guard and each home has its own private gate. I'd say you were doing it big, Doctor. But I'm impressed by how humble you are. Riley is very lucky to have you."

"I'm the lucky one." The doctor rubbed Kalia's lips and his dick sprang to life. "Donnie Brasco wants a kiss,' he pointed to his dick.

Kalia slid down the length of him and began pleasing him the way he taught her. He came in her mouth once more and then told her goodnight. Normally, she would have been pissed off from being dismissed but she learned that this was simply the way he was. Plus, she couldn't wait to get back to her room so she could talk to Colby. The doctor was cool and Kalia was in very deep like with him but her heart belonged to the young prince in Atlanta who had swept her off her feet.

The little red notification light on her cell phone blinked. She either had a missed call or a text. Regardless of which one, it would have to wait until she showered. It felt nice and cool in her room so Kalia opted to air dry instead of using one of the thick, plush towels. She crawled between the cool sheets and picked up her cell phone. She had three missed calls. One from both Anika and Riley and the other from Colby. Since the girls never kept her on the phone long, she called them back first.

Riley answered her phone on the first ring. "Hey girl, what you doing? Why you didn't answer me and Nika's call?"

"Girl I was swimming in this big ass garden tub, getting my bathe on. I think I'm in love with this place," Kalia lied.

"I figured as much. Anika is in the tub now."

"What's up, though?" Kalia loved her girls but she didn't want to be on the phone with them when she could be talking to her new boo.

"Why you rushing me off the phone? Let me find out you got a fine ass Frenchman over there."

Kalia laughed at her friend. "Girl, your ass is crazy. I wasn't rushing you. We can talk, just not too long. I wanted to return my mother's call before she left for Bible study. She called while I was in the tub, too."

"Your mom called? Man, that's cool. I hoped she wouldn't be mad forever. Anyway, Anika and I want to do the whole Parisian tourist thing tomorrow. You down?"

"You know I am but I have my internship. Some of us must work, remember? I'm not here on vacation like you and Nik." Kalia hoped she didn't sound bitter to her friend.

"Girl, your ass doesn't work. You call filing a few files and then going to the best restaurants for lunch with Daddy, work? I don't even think so."

"Laughing my butt off. You're right. Yeah, I'm down. I need to clear it with your father though."

"Already did. Daddy said we could all go. So, you know what that means don't you? We're going to do some...."

"Shopping." Both girls yelled at the same time.

"Cool beans. Well let me call my mom and I'll see you guys for breakfast in the morning. Tell Anika goodnight if you call her back."

"I will. Goodnight, Sis."

"Goodnight."

Kalia couldn't wait to get Riley off the phone. The clock on the bedside table said that it was ten-fifteen p.m. That meant it was four-fifteen p.m. in Atlanta. Colby would be on his way to the gym now. She scrolled through her contacts and pressed his name when she saw it and waited for her phone to connect with his. *I need to put his ass on speed dial*, she thought, twirling the ends of her hair around her finger. His cell phone rang five times and then went to voice mail.

Damn.

Sad that he didn't answer, Kalia decided to call it a night. She was spent from being with Dr. Sutton earlier. He made her come four times in a row. A record for her. The man's tongue was almost as long and thick as his dick and he knew exactly which spot to stroke to produce the creamy nectar that he loved to taste. She fluffed her pillows and sank against them, letting the comfort and peace envelop her. Two hours later she was awakened by the shrill ring of her cell phone.

"Hello," she said groggily.

"Hey, Babe. Were you asleep? I didn't mean to wake you."

"Hey, Boo. I guess I was and didn't realize it. How are you?"

"I'm chill. I can call you tomorrow if you want."

"Nah. You good. I was trying to catch you before you went to the gym earlier. I hate I missed you."

"Me too. I had some errands to run for my mom and left my phone at her house. I thought I lost the damned thing for a minute."

"Oh, wow. Glad you didn't. I don't know what I would do if I couldn't talk to you while I was here."

"I'd have to fly over to be with you then. Nothing is going to stop me from getting revenge."

"What did you say? Your phone was cutting out. Did you say revenge?"

Fuck. "Nah. I said nothing is going to stop me from getting to my girlfriend."

"Oh, so I'm your girlfriend now, am I?"

"Yes, you are."

"Hmm. When did this happen?"

"This morning when I woke up and realized that I was in love with you."

"What? Wait. You're what?"

"I'm in love with you, Kalia. I know that you may think I'm crazy because we haven't known one another long, but I feel like I've known you my whole life. You have my heart, Lia. I want us to be together. Eventually, I want to make you my wife." Colby rolled his eyes and snickered quietly.

"Oh, baby. I love you, too. I wanted to tell you but I was scared. And I would love to be the future Mrs. Byron."

Colby and Kalia talked on the phone for an hour and then he let her go so she could get some rest. The six-hour time difference favored him, not her. It was after midnight in Paris. Not that he really cared. He had a few surprises in store for his girlfriend. His dick got hard thinking about them.

At nine o'clock the next morning, Kalia met Anika, Riley and Dr. Sutton in the hotel lobby and he escorted them to breakfast. The girls talked excitedly about what they wanted to see and do that day. Anika was an architecture major and wanted to see all the beautiful, historical structures of Paris. Riley and Kalia didn't care about any of that. They wanted to shop until they dropped. The first attraction they saw was The Louvre. It was the world's largest museum. Anika was awed by the classic structure and clean lines of the amazing building.

"Are you crying?" Riley asked Anika.

"No, but I do have tears in my eyes. This is such an awe-inspiring sight. Look at God. You know it had to be Him that gave someone the wit and creativity to come up with this and the other landmarks. Simply amazing."

"Ol' cry baby, ass." Kalia mumbled.

They toured the Luxembourg Gardens, Notre Dame Cathedral, The Pont Alexander III Bridge and a few other notable sights with a tourist. Dr. Sutton, didn't like the pace of the tour guide and suggested they take the city on by themselves.

"That sounds like a great idea, Daddy. I was struggling to understand that joker anyway."

"You should have stayed in French class then, isn't that right, Dr. Sutton?" Anika volunteered.

"Indeed. Let's go, ladies. We have a lot of area to cover."

Riley grabbed Anika's hand with her left hand and her father's hand with the right one. "Get Kalia's hand, Daddy. We need to stay linked up. I don't want us to get abducted and end up a part of a sex slave ring. I saw a special on Sixty Minutes about that. Uh huh."

"You watch too much TV daughter," her father said laughing.

They taxied down the Champs-Elysees and did some shopping along the way. It was Kalia's first time walking inside a Louis Vuitton store. The good doctor bought the three girls a new handbag and matching wallet and got one for his wife also. He picked up a belt and a hat for himself, and that brought his total to over fifteen thousand dollars. Moisture began to form between Kalia's legs as she watched him swipe his American Express Black Card. There was something about a man with money that drove her wild.

Next, they went down Rue Saint Honore'. Prada. Givenchy. Marc Jacobs. Sheer excitement from being in her favorite shops were going to cause juices to start running down her legs while they shopped. Dr. Sutton didn't bat an eye when the girls held up a dress, pair of shoes or anything. It was an orgasmic experience. She fidgeted in the car seat after coming out of those exclusive shops. The car service sent over a short Rolls Royce Phantom limo. Kalia and Dr. Sutton sat in the back with all the packages and Riley and Anika sat in the middle row. Sensing her frustration, Dr. Sutton moved the bags over her lap so he could slide his finger under her skirt.

Kalia's legs parted ever so slightly, allowing him easy access to her hot, wet center. She had to close her eyes and bite down on the inside of her mouth to keep from screaming out in pleasure. He flicked her clit with his middle finger and pressed down on it, rubbing in a circular motion. A few more strokes and Kalia was going to come.

"Look." Riley shouted. "The Eiffel Tower. Can we get out Daddy?" Riley whipped her head around to the back seat and her father sat there frozen with a smile on his face.

"Of course, Darling. Tell the driver to find a place to park." Reluctantly, he removed his hand from the love glove and whispered to Kalia "We'll finish this soon. Trust me."

They got out of the car and walked up the steps to the impressive tower. Dr. Sutton snapped pictures of the trio as they posed, made faces and horsed around. When they got hungry, he suggested lunch inside the Eiffel Tower and they rode the elevator to the third level. During lunch, each girl took pictures of the city from their elevated view. This was something to brag about back home.

"Would you girls like to see the city from the top?" Dr. Sutton was creating an opportunity to get his rocks off.

"Un huh."

"No way."

Both Anika and Riley feared heights and wouldn't take an elevator higher than five stories. He counted on them declining before he asked.

"Would either of you be offended if I took Kalia to see it then? Gustave Eiffel, the designer, had a private apartment at the top of the tower. For the longest time no one was allowed to see it but I can."

"Go ahead, Daddy. Anika and I will wait here for you guys. We saw some desserts we want to try."

Dr. Sutton and Kalia got on the elevator with a few other people but not many. He rubbed her butt as the elevator climbed higher and higher. It stopped a few times along the way, letting the others off. Once they got to the top, Dr. Sutton produced a key and walked Kalia to the door of the apartment.

"How'd you get that?" She asked.

"I know people," he stated.

Inside, they hurried over to the sofa with neither of them speaking and they began to kiss and touch like a couple of teenagers.

When their lips finally separated, Kalia removed her blouse and took off her bra. She shook her titties to further entice Dr. Sutton. He took one of the twin beauties in each of his hands and began licking and sucking her nipples.

"Mmm, I love the way you do that, Doctor."

He didn't say anything back to her, choosing to let his actions, do all the talking. When the nipple he was sucking on got erect, he moved to the next one, enjoying it almost as much. For a few minutes, he switched back and forth between Kalia's nipples, as she cooed in pleasure and squirmed in front of him. He could tell she was turned on and they both anticipated that there was more pleasure to be had the lower he went.

Kalia stood up and turned around so the doctor could unzip her skirt and help her take it off. Because they had to rejoin the other's, he folded it neatly and laid it to the side so it wouldn't get wrinkled. He pulled her in front of him and started in again on her nipples.

"That's enough on the twins. I want to feel your mouth on my pussy."

'Yes, Ma'am." He said, grinning mischievously.

He began licking his way down her body starting with the sensitive valley between her breasts and proceeded down her firm, tight belly. When he reached the tip of her nether lips, he paused and inhaled her essence. He could see the cream between her lips and his dick got harder. Sitting her down on the sofa, he parted her lips with his fingers and saw the dripping nectar that he was ready to taste.

Slowly he licked up and down inside her pussy before wrapping his lips around her clit, sucking it out from under the hood. She moaned as his finger entered her, curling upwards to rest on her G-spot.

"Please, Doctor…" She whimpered in a childlike voice.

"Please what, baby."

"Fuck me."

"Not yet."

Kalia's eyes were partially closed but she saw his face, with his mouth and chin glistening from her juices. His tongue assaulted her pussy once more and he was sucking the clit like it was a small dick.

"Ooohhh, suck this pussy, Daddy. Gosh, you eat me so good. I'm coming baby. I'm com-ing."

"Turn over on your belly and put this under you," he said, handing her a pillow after her spasms subsided.

Her pretty, round ass was prominently displayed and her pussy dripped from pleasure. He fingered her pussy and used the juices to lube her ass. He licked and tongued her asshole as she squealed and moaned and pushed back against his face. Kalia went crazy. No one had ever licked her ass before and the new sensations almost drove her over the edge. With her first orgasm so fresh, she was still very sensitive and quite close to a second one.

"Oh fuck, Doctor. I'm gonna come again. Puh-lease make me come."

Dr. Sutton shoved four fingers inside Kalia's pussy and his tongue invaded her ass at the same time, causing her to explode in another volcanic eruption. Since she was already at the height of satisfaction, he used his cream covered fingers to lube his hard dick and he placed it at the entrance of her puckered butt hole. He centered it and thrust firmly inside her, sighing in joy, feeling her tightness around him. Kalia cried out in a little pain but pleasure quickly took over.

Long deep strokes penetrated her as he eased inside inch by inch. He moved slowly at first, allowing her body to get used to the size of him, then he picked up the pace. His hard dick rammed in and out of her tight hole. Her pussy juices ran down her thighs and Dr. Sutton played with her clit. He stroked it with the same tempo he used while fucking her ass.

The doctor was almost ready to come as well. He began pumping faster and she matched his increased speed. Kalia bounced her ass on his dick as she threw it back at him. She was moaning and sobbing at the immense pleasure she was receiving from the doctors' big dick as it continued to fill her up.

"I'm coming again, Doctor. Come with me, baby."

He obliged. Dr. Sutton could feel his hot come shoot from his body to hers. Kalia could feel the heat going in as her own juices poured out. A few more strokes and Dr. Sutton had shot a huge load inside his young paramour. Satisfied, he laid her gently on her belly until their breathing evened out. Without saying any words, they used some baby wipes Kalia had in her purse to clean up and they dressed. Kalia wrapped the used wipes in some paper to toss out when they got back downstairs.

They joined the girls who had picked up some cute Italian tourists and had dessert with them. Back at the hotel, Kalia showered and changed and rested up for the loving that she would receive in a few short hours. She had dinner with her friends in Anika's room after her nap and then she was back in her suite. Dr. Sutton took his time with her and made love to every inch of her body. She imagined that it was Colby stroking her instead of the good doctor and that served to make her come harder.

The internship and Paris trip was coming to a close. Kalia gained a new-found respect for shrinks. In addition, she learned how to suck dick better and please a man in every way possible. She couldn't wait to perform her new skills on Colby. Dr. Sutton had created a real head doctor.

THE HONEYMOON STAGE

The light at the top of the Bank of America Tower in Atlanta could be seen clearly from the plane as it made a slow descent onto the tarmac. It was a welcoming beacon of possibilities for Kalia because in a matter of minutes, she would see Colby. Kalia had a few friends who had found love via internet dating sites but thought it was all a bunch of crap. How could a person fall in love simply by talking to a man using instant messages, texts, or even talking on the phone? Falling in love required being in someone's presence she thought. But now, she understood. Even though she and Colby spent time together before she left for Paris, it wasn't much. The two of them forged an intimate connection from talking on the phone.

While she was in Paris, they spoke on the phone daily. Colby was interested in Kalia in every way, not only sexually. She knew that because when she suggested that they have phone sex he turned her down. He said that he wanted to get to know her without adding sex to the equation because once that happened, it changed things.

"Let's take it slow. We have plenty of time for that," he told her.

That made her fall even harder. There wasn't a minute that went by that she didn't think about him. He was on her mind all the time. Even when Dr. Sutton was eating her pussy, all she could imagine was Colby's tongue in place of the older man's. When she was in North Carolina at school, she had a few lovers. Some because she really liked them, others because they were beneficial to her plans. But Colby was different. She genuinely adored him for who he was and not what he had.

He was kind and loving and treated her like the queen she felt like she was. Him having megabucks, was a bonus. As a matter of fact, he was coming to the airport to pick her up. She told Riley and Dr. Sutton that she would be spending a few days at her 'cousins' house when they got back to Atlanta. Truth is, she planned to spend those days with Colby at his apartment.

The overhead light came on signaling the passengers to put on their seatbelts. Kalia closed the book that she was supposed to be reading. She hadn't read one word of it. Once she opened it, her thoughts immediately went to her man. Dr. Sutton also made it hard for her to concentrate because he was fingering her under her lap blanket, making her come a couple of times. She returned the favor by jacking him off. The good doctor came in her palm loving the fact that she licked even the smallest drop of his come off her hand. Riley and Anika were knocked out, sedated by sleeping pills to help take the edge off the turbulent flight. They were oblivious to what was going down in the first-class cocoons two rows behind.

A pretty flight attendant came by, lightly tapping on the pod doors to ask passengers for last minute requests. The knock jarred the doctor awake. He yawned and rolled his head to look at Kalia.

"You have pleased me well. I like you. I'm sure I don't have to tell you that discretion is still key now that we are back in Atlanta, do I?"

"Not at all. I enjoyed being with you, Dr. Sutton. I've learned things from you that I'm sure can't be taught in any class room. I'm looking forward to staying at the house with you all. That should be very…. interesting."

"Indeed, it shall be, dear girl."

Riley and Anika woke up as the plane touched down and Kalia laughed when she heard one of them squeal when the plane jerked. Kalia knew that Riley hated that part with a passion but hell, once the plane was within ten feet of the ground, Kalia didn't trip. If it crashed when they got that close, they'd still live. The plane taxied down the runway slowly headed towards the terminal. The first-class passengers were released first when they opened the doors.

"I hope you didn't mind sharing the pod with Daddy, Kalia. He snores too loudly for me to sleep."

"It was okay, Riley. We talked a little bit and I read for the better part of the flight. I was too excited to sleep anyway."

"Hmmm, I wonder why?" Anika giggled. "Colby must have been on someone's mind."

Blushing, Kalia nodded her head. "Yeah he was. Guys I swear I think I'm in love with him." She didn't reveal that she already was.

"I can see that. He's all you talk about and when you hear his name your eyes light up. You start giggling like a school girl and your black ass turns all red."

"Whatever. But is it really that obvious?"

"Yep. Stevie Wonder called me and said he saw it, too."

"I see you got jokes as usual Riley. Let's catch the plane train so that we can get to baggage claim. My boo is waiting for me."

Fifteen minutes later Kalia stood in the international passenger pick up area, waiting for Colby. Dr. Sutton's hired car was waiting for them as soon as they got outside and the chauffer loaded their luggage quickly.

"Are you sure you don't want to ride with us, Lia? Your um, cousin can pick you up from the house," Riley offered.

"No, I'm good. I got off the phone with her when I was in the restroom and she is coming. She was on the domestic terminal side," Kalia lied.

That was ten minutes ago. A lot of people had trouble navigating the loops and turns at Hartsfield-Jackson Airport and did end up lost. This was one of the busiest airports in the United States and unless you came out here every day, it was impossible to know all the ins and outs. Kalia hoped that Colby had gotten lost or hit a pocket of traffic versus forgetting to come pick her up altogether. She called him over ten times and sent as many texts but he didn't reply to either. 1:21p.m. Almost 25 minutes later and no word from him. Just as she was about to call a taxi, he pulled up in front of her.

"Sorry I'm so late, babe. There was an accident on I-85 by Grady Hospital. Traffic is backed up all the way to the Lenox Road exit."

"It's okay, Colby. I'd wait for you forever."

He placed her luggage in the trunk and held the door open for her to get inside the car. Expecting to get on the highway as soon as they left off airport property, Kalia was surprised to see him taking a different route.

"Where are we going?"

"I have a surprise for you. Since I was late, I figured I had some making up to do."

The couple went to a beautiful restaurant in College Park called the Pecan and had a fine meal. The lamb was gently prepared and the red wine was refreshing to their pallets. They talked about her trip and the things that he did while she was away. They drank, laughed and had a good time. After dinner Colby took Kalia to the Marriott Hotel a mile from the restaurant. He didn't take her suitcases out the car and he didn't have any bags either. She noticed that when they got inside, he didn't stop by the front desk to check in.

"Are we coming to visit someone?" She inquired.

"Not really. Wait, you'll see."

The elevator stopped on their floor and Colby escorted her to the room. He took a key card out of his pocket and when he opened the door, he stood to the side and ushered her in.

"For you my love."

Kalia saw the rose petals on the floor by the light of all the candles that illuminated the room. She walked inside the room, following the trail that led to the bed. There was a heart made of rose petals on the white plush comforter and Kalia's name spelled out in the center of it.

"You did all of this for me, babe?" She was in awe. This man was trying to get her sprung and it was working.

"Yes. I wanted to do something special for you. I know that you had a fancy suite in Paris but I wasn't there so it couldn't have been that good," he joked.

"Colby, this is amazing. Thank you, baby."

Kalia reached up and wrapped her arms around Colby's neck and kissed him passionately on the lips. He pulled her close and deepened the kiss, intensifying it with each stroke of his velvet tongue. Their tongues wrestled and explored one another, familiarizing themselves as they licked and sucked. Colby tore his mouth from his girlfriend's and allowed his tender kisses to travel down her neck, shoulders and the tops of her breasts.

"Sweetie, hold on," Colby said when Kalia began to unzip his jeans.

"What is it?"

"I want to make love to you. Believe me I do, but I think that we need to wait. I know it may sound corny but I think we should."

"Are you serious, baby? Why did you get the room then?"

"Because, I thought that it was the right time to…for us to..." He feigned shyness.

"Colby, I love you baby. This *is* the right time for us. I want you. Don't you want me?"

"You know I do. Let me show you how much."

Colby began kissing Kalia again and this time he laid her down on the bed. As they rolled and kissed, clothes miraculously came off. Before Kalia knew it, she was completely naked but Colby was still fully dressed.

"I know how to make you feel even better when I make love to you."

Nervously, Kalia sat up, thinking that he was talking about drugs. "H-how?" she stammered.

"This," he said, holding up a blind fold.

"I don't get it."

"If you can't see what I'm getting ready to do to you, then you have to rely solely on your senses. This will increase your sense of touch, taste and smell. Are you ready?"

She nodded and he blindfolded her.

"One more thing. You can't touch me either. I have free reign over you tonight."

Excited, Kalia laid back and smiled when he tied her hands together with a bandana.

"Open wide" he commanded.

Kalia opened her mouth and stuck out her tongue in time to feel his large dick touch her lips.

83

"Make it wet. Spit on it. Don't worry about stroking it. I can do that. Suck it."

His dick smelled like strawberries. She liked that. *A clean man.* Using the skills, she learned in Paris, Kalia licked up and down the shaft, spitting on it and sucking it hard from tip to base. Her head bobbed back and forth.

"Ah, yeah. That's it. Suck this dick, Lia."

Hearing her name gave her confidence to take more of him in her mouth and she increased the speed.

"Oh, you want to do it like that, huh? Alright then."

Colby shoved all his meat in her mouth and Kalia gagged. His dick was hitting the back of her tonsils, activating her gag reflex. She tried to take her hands out of bondage but they were bound tightly. The more she struggled, the faster and harder Colby drilled her mouth.

"I'm about to let this shit go," he growled as hot semen shot into her mouth and on her face when she backed up. "I got something else for you."

Kalia was pulled to the middle of the bed and she felt the weight of the bed, dip once, then again. *Was there was someone else in the room?* Strong hands held her legs open and Kalia felt a hot tongue on her clit. She jumped when the tongue circled her clit but relaxed as Colby began to show her his expertise eating pussy.

"Oh yea, babe. That feels so good. You're a master," she complimented.

The bed dipped again and Kalia smelled strawberries again. Colby? His dick slid in her mouth again and she started sucking.

If Colby is fucking my mouth, who's eating me out? Is this a three-some? She thought. Her full mouth prevented her from asking.

She was feeling very good and the tongue was sending her over the edge. Just as she was about to come, she felt her hips lift and a soft pillow was placed under her butt. The hot tongue licked her pussy and her ass hole. She moaned loudly with the dick in her mouth. Without warning, an extra wide, long dick shoved its way inside Kalia's ass and rammed her fiercely. The dick in her dry anus hurt like hell and when Kalia screamed out, she sounded like a deaf mute.

A strangled moan filled the air. It was coming from the person whose dick was in her ass. He was about to come. Kalia didn't know who he was and furthermore, couldn't tell if this unknown man had used a condom. She could tell by the way he pumped though that he was coming and he didn't pull out. Colby, or whoever's dick she had in her mouth also released a powerful nut and she gagged on the semen as it went down her throat. Moments later, the bed shifted and she was alone.

"Here, drink this," Colby said without removing the blindfold from her eyes. "It'll help you sleep."

When Kalia woke up, the beautiful sunlight filled the room and she felt very refreshed. Surprisingly, her body wasn't sore the way she expected it to be. The way it always was after anal sex. The room looked differently in the light of day. It looked more like home versus a hotel room. Stretching, Kalia sat up and threw her legs over the side of the bed. She was about to stand up when the door burst open.

"Hey, you're awake. About damned time, sleepy head."

Riley? What in the hell was she doing here?

"Ri, what's going on?" Kalia was in the twilight zone.

"That's what I've been waiting on you to wake up for so I could find out."

"What do you mean?"

"Girl, you been asleep almost three days. Daddy thought he was going to have to call 9-1-1 and Mommy was pacing the floor back and forth. I think she wore a hole in the carpet."

"How did I... where's Colby?" The last she remembered he was fucking her brains out.

"Colby brought you home. He said that you got sick after dinner and passed out in the car right after you gave him our address. He packed you upstairs. I put on your pajamas. Well, Nika helped, too. But you've been sleep since then."

"After dinner? So me and Colby didn't go to the hotel?"

"Girl, you're tripping. He brought you here right after dinner."

Wow. I dreamt all of that then? Whew, thank you God. That explains why my body doesn't hurt.

"Well um, I guess I'll get up and get moving. I'm sure I have to things to do."

"Nora, our housekeeper, sent your clothes out to the dry cleaners that were in your suit case. You'll find them all hanging in the chifforobe over there. Also, me and Mommy bought you some undies and things while we were out. She thinks it's cool having another daughter in the house."

"That was sweet of you two. Thank you."

"No problem. I'll let you shower and dress. I told them your 'cousin' stood you up and that's how you ended up with Colby. Go along with it if they ask about it," Riley said getting up to leave. "Oh, and Lia?"

"Yeah?"

"I'm glad you're here. I love you."

"I love you, too."

A very happy Kalia got up and showered. She laughed out loud at the dream she had. It felt so real nevertheless. *I'll ask Colby what happened when I see him again, she mumbled.* Once she showered and dressed Kalia called Colby and made a date with him. She couldn't wait to ask him what happened. He held all the missing pieces to the puzzle. Their date was that night at seven-thirty so she dressed carefully because she wanted to impress him. At seven-fifteen, he called her.

"Hey, I have to cancel our date. My mom is sick and I need to tend to her. I'll call you as soon as I can."

A few weeks passed with no word from Colby. Dr. Sutton noticed a forlorn Kalia and asked her to come to his office one evening. Riley, Anika and their moms went to the Fox Theater to see Dream Girls. Kalia passed on the invitation, pretending to have a headache.

"Are you, okay my young lover?" Dr. Sutton, patting his lap so Kalia could go sit there. "Tell Daddy what's wrong."

"Well, you know I met this guy I really like. We were supposed to go out three weeks ago and he cancelled because of an emergency. I haven't heard from him since. I called him the other day and it said his phone was disconnected. I thought we were working on something."

"Baby Doll, young men don't know how to deal with emotions as young women do. The emergency may have taken a toll on him and he's trying to figure out how to process his feelings. Give him a little time. I'm sure he'll come around."

"You think so?"

"I know so. And if he doesn't, he's stupid and you didn't need him anyway."

"Awe, Daddy, you always know how to make me feel good," she cooed.

"Yes," he said seductively "I know how to make you feel even better."

"Oh yes, please do, Daddy. Make little Lia feel really good."

Dr. Sutton slid his hand under Kalia's maxi dress and moved her panties to the side so he could bury his fingers in her snatch. Two, then three fingers fucked her and she writhed in his lap. Twirling her hips over his groin made him hard and he lifted her so he could unzip his pants. She reached inside his boxers and let his dick spring free. Raising her dress up, he kept her panties to the side and slid his dick in her pussy, grinding and pumping alternately. Kalia leaned over his desk and gave him full view of her ass.

The good doctor slapped her ass and put his thumb in the hole. It was tender and Kalia winced in pain but let him continue. Soon pleasure overtook her and she yelled.

"I'm coming, Daddy. Fuck this pussy baby. Make me come."

He pumped faster and threw his head back, leaning it on the soft leather of his executive chair.

"Awe, shit. I feel an eruption coming. Drink the hot lava, baby," he said, pulling out of Kalia and positioning her on the floor. She was completely under his desk, on her knees, sucking his dick.

"Ooh, baby. This big dick is delicious," she said, slurping.

There was laughter in the hallway and then Mrs. Sutton's voice.

"Okay, let me tell Donald."

Kalia froze when the door opened.

"Honey, the four of us are back from the play."

"Did you enjoy yourselves?" Dr. Sutton asked as if nothing was wrong.

"Absolutely. I wanted to tell you that we're going to Alicia's for a bit. We stopped here so I could get my slippers. Those heals were killing me. Will you be okay without us?"

"No worries. I'm being entertained."

"Good, dear. I love to hear that. We'll see you later."

"Enjoy, my love." He blew her a kiss.

"Oh, and thank you, Kalia. I couldn't suck him off tonight. My jaws are tired from this morning. And make sure you swallow all the come, Dear. I simply abhor semen in his drawers."

Check mate.

BORN BAD

Weeks had passed since Colby last spoke with Kalia. He liked her but he had to let her stew for a while. Keep her guessing.

"Move your ass," he yelled to a driver sitting at a green light.

Driving through Atlanta traffic irritated him. He turned on Memorial Drive towards the cemetery where his father was laid to rest. He was going to place flowers on his grave. Although he'd never met him, he felt close to him. His mother abandoned him when he was a baby and his father died a year after he was born. Left an orphan, he was raised by his aunt. She was the reason he cancelled the date with Kalia a few weeks ago.

Up ahead, he could see the cemetery to the left of him and he slowed down to make his turn. Once he got on the grounds, he took the familiar route that led to the section where his father was buried. The sun was shining brightly when he got out of the car. In a matter of moments, he was kneeled before his dad's tombstone.

"Hey old man, I brought you some fresh flowers. Monty sends her love. We miss you. She talks about you daily. She's told me so many stories about you that I feel like I was there when you did most of that stuff. The last time I was here I told you that I was going to meet someone special. Well Dad, I did. Her name is Kalia and she's the one. I have big plans in store for her. She's the one."

Colby spent another few minutes there in silence before heading home. Cinnamon and sugar wafted through the air when he walked through the front door of his house.

"Monty," he sang out. "Smells like you're baking cinnamon rolls for me."

"Of course, I am, baby boy. Come sit down. They're hot out the oven."

"Wow, they're huge. You spoil me, Monty."

The woman giggled.

"You have been calling me that your whole life. I never get tired of hearing it."

"I hope not. You're my mom slash aunty. My Monty. You're all I have in this world."

"Only until you meet that special someone."

"Speaking of which, I met her."

"Oh, did you now? And what's she like?"

"Gorgeous, smart. Most definitely a gold-digger though. But it's all good. I'm looking forward to the possibilities."

"I'm sure you are, Dear. Tell me about your visit," she inquired.

"It was cool. Thanks to you, I feel as if I knew my dad. I know he wasn't perfect, and I thank you for telling me the truth about him, but I still believe that he and I would have had a great relationship."

"I know that you all would have."

"Sometimes I wish things were different. It's not that I don't love you and appreciate you, I wish he was here, too."

"No need to explain. I understand exactly how you feel. There's not a day that goes by that I don't miss my brother. It was the two of us for so long. We protected each other. Yes, we did. He was the best brother a sister could ask for. That's why it was so important for me to raise you the way I know he would have. Education was always paramount with him."

"I know. School starts back in a few days. The girl, Kalia, she'll be attending Tech too. This may be the best semester yet."

"You make sure that you are concentrating more on your studies than you are on those nappy headed girls."

He laughed out loud. "Kalia has good hair."

"Humph, there's no such thing. All of our hair is good hair."

Colby paused and looked at his aunt seriously.

"Thank you for always being here for me, Monty. I love you very much."

"I love you too, Son."

The pair sat at the table enjoying the hot rolls and ice-cold milk. Monty, whose real name is Barbara, looked upon her nephew lovingly. With eyes like his father's, she hoped his heart was the same. Finding out that she was going to be an aunt was so exciting. But knowing he was going to be a father was everything to her brother. Unfortunately, he didn't live long enough to see his son grow. Absentmindedly, she took a sip of her drink. Colby was still talking and had no clue she had zoned out for a moment.

"I'm looking forward to being with Kalia."

"Is that right?"

"Yes, Ma'am. I have great things in store for her."

"I'm sure you do. You're such a kind young man. Your father would be proud of you."

"You think so?"

"I know so. I remember when you were a small boy and the little Monroe girl down the street got her first puppy. You were so happy for her. But then she didn't want you to play with him and that made you very angry. I'll never forget the day you stole him and brought him here."

"I remember that, too," he chuckled. "She looked for him for a week straight."

"Yes, she did. I was tickled pink to hear that little annoying animal squealing when you put a match to his paws."

"You should have seen her face when she opened her front door to see him hanging from the lamp post in their front yard. I can still hear her scream," Colby laughed.

"I discovered then that you were the spitting image of your father. I don't think that I've ever been prouder of you than I was in that moment."

"Well you know what they say, like father like son. But you ain't seen nothing yet."

MAJOR PAINS

Choosing a college major could be a royal pain for some but not for Kalia. Having worked with Dr. Sutton and familiarizing herself with his practice, she knew exactly what she wanted to do. She was going to major in psychology. Dr. Sutton was a psychiatrist but Kalia didn't want to take up all those science classes, attend medical school or do a four-year residency. Her plan was to get to the money as quickly as possible and working with Dr. Sutton had given her a head start. The good doctor paid her generously for every special client she "serviced" and the client always followed-up with a handsome tip at the end of each session.

When school began, she was exited. The education she received in Paris was priceless and Kalia was determined to have the same, high-end, high-paying clientele as her mentor. After returning from abroad, she remained at the Sutton's home until she could get into a dorm room. Mrs. Sutton and Riley took advantage of their wealth and jet-set around the globe. Riley wanted her friend to tag along but Kalia declined, citing that she had to stay behind and work on things with her family. No one in Kalia's family cared much about what she had going on. The last time any of them were together was right before the Paris trip. Her father had made it crystal clear that since she didn't want to be a part of the family then she was unwelcomed in their home. Although she did call her mother periodically, it was more out of duty than love. Her family was living the life that they chose. Meanwhile, Kalia led the life she desired.

The Atlanta weather was perfect the first day of classes and continued in that manner for the rest of the week. As much as she initially hated having to transfer schools and return home, Kalia was glad at the turn of events. Regardless of where she graduated, it was in the cards for her to be successful no matter what. The professors at the university fawned over Kalia's brains and beauty as she worked hard to stand out among the masses. She shared a couple of classes with both Colby and Riley and she had no problems showing either of them up when it came to the course work.

It was almost a month since the nightmare, as Kalia began to call it, that she finally met with Colby for lunch. This was her chance to ask him what happened that night.

"Babe, I had the strangest dream the night we had dinner after I returned from Paris."

"Oh, yeah? Do tell," he said, listening intently, resting his chin on his palm with his elbow on the table.

"Well, in my dream, we had dinner exactly how it was. I remember our conversation vividly. But afterwards, we went to a hotel and we started to kiss. You hesitated at first but then we got hot and heavy. I was blind-folded and then we got busy."

"Sounds like my kind of dream," he chuckled.

"Silly goose. Anyway, I think it ended up being a couple of people in the bed with us but I didn't know who because I couldn't see anyone. I could only feel and smell. Someone smelled like strawberries. I thought it was you."

He stared at her plate with a weird look on his face.

"Why are you looking at my plate like that?" She questioned.

"Well, you know they say your dreams are associated with what you eat. I'm checking to see what you eat so that when you tell me about your next dream I'll know what not to eat."

"Whatever," she said playfully. "It felt so real. But then I woke up and I was at the Sutton's, comfortable in bed where Riley said I had been for three days."

"Yeah, you had gotten pretty sick at the restaurant. I didn't know what to do so I called Monty who said to take you home. She said that you were probably experiencing something like delayed jet-lag. I called to check on you several times and Mrs. Sutton told me that you were resting."

"Thank you so much. It was so weird to me. It all seemed so real."

"I imagine so. None of that happened, however," he said, changing the subject quickly.

Kalia hated being dismissed and was about to tell him as much when a young lady walked over to their table.

"Excuse me, Sir. But I couldn't help but notice how fine you are and felt like you needed to know me. I'm Tam and you are?" She extended her hand towards Colby. Kalia slapped it away.

"Taken, bitch. Can't you see that he's having dinner with his woman? Rude ass. You will get knocked the fuck out in here."

The woman laughed and stepped closer to Colby but said nothing in return.

"Kalia. Language." Colby censured. "What have I told you about that?"

"How in the hell are you going to check me when this bitch walked over here and disrespected me by trying to get at you? I'm not the one to be fucked with and if you're going to be with me then you need to respect me too, nigga."

"First, don't ever call me that again. Second, Kalia I'd like you to meet my cousin Tamara who happens to do this every time we are in a public place."

"Hi, I'm Tam. Nice to meet you."

It took a moment for his words to register. Kalia looked at the bombshell who stood before her with her hand outstretched and reluctantly, she took it.

"I am so embarrassed. Please forgive me. I'm Kalia. Oh my gosh, this is awkward."

"No worries. I'm glad to see that you reacted the way you did. That means you care. She's a keeper, fam."

"Meh, she a'ight," he laughed. "I may keep her. If she stops cussing like a sailor."

Tam giggled. "Well, I have to go. My lunch date has arrived. It was a pleasure meeting you, Kalia. Bye, Bighead."

"Bye, smelly cat."

The couple sat down and looked at one another. Tears welled up in Kalia's eyes.

"Are those tears?" Colby asked, reaching across the table to wipe her eyes.

"Yes," she sniffed.

"Why? She's really my cousin. Like if I were to need blood or an organ she could probably give it to me."

"It's not that. It's…well, I didn't realize how much I loved you until I was faced with losing you."

"Babe, no woman can walk up and take me from you. If it's that easy, then you don't need to be with me or any man like that for that matter. I'm a one-woman man and I know that you are a one-man woman."

At that, all she could do was smile and nod. Lunch continued uneventfully and then they left. Kalia was quieter than usual in the car.

"What's up? Are you giving me the silent treatment?" He inquired.

"No. I'm thinking. We have such a great relationship and we do so much together but I need to know, where do you see us heading?"

Colby killed the ignition and turned to face Kalia.

"I thought I made that clear. While I'm not ready for marriage today, I do see us getting married. There are times at night that I envision you swollen with my child and I must be honest, that makes me happy. I know I don't say it often but I love you and believe it or not, I have big plans for you."

"For us."

He leaned over and pulled her to him, caressing her body. Colby gave her the side-eye behind her back. A wicked smile formed at the corners of his mouth. Marriage was the last thing he considered and if he was it most definitely wouldn't be with her. She was a conniving, gold-digging whore and he was aware of all her lascivious acts because he had her investigated. But it didn't matter what she did because in the end, it would all work together to serve his purpose.

"Babe, you're so good to me," she admitted.

"You make it easy for me to be," he lied. "Do you have to go to the office today?" He knew she did before he asked her.

"Unfortunately, I do. Dr. Sutton will be out of the country for two weeks and we have a lot to do."

"Are you going with him?"

"No. Why would I? I'm only his intern."

"I forgot, babe. You do so much it's difficult to believe that you're not paid for all your hard work."

"Awe, you're such a sweetie. Can we get together tonight?"

"Not tonight. Matter-of-fact, I'm going to be out of town for the next few days. Monty is going to visit Tam's mom in Savannah. We'll be back in three or four days."

Disappointed, Kalia replied, "I understand. Well you guys have a good time and I will see you when you return."

A few moments later, Colby dropped Kalia off in front of the Dr. Sutton's prestigious Buckhead office. Seeing the grand structure put a smile on her face. One day, she was going to have an office like this. The old her would have tried to finagle a building out him by using some of the information she had. But Kalia was aware of who she was interning for. Regardless of the unique way he handled his clientele, the doctor was discrete and extremely professional. He was also a force to be reckoned with. Dr. Sutton could have her killed and disposed of without a trace. His ties to the underworld didn't go unnoticed. She did what she was told and kept her mouth shut. Besides, he was too generous with her and if she wanted anything all she had to do was ask.

Lily, the doctor's administrative assistant was seated at her desk reading a magazine when Kalia walked in. The older woman looked down on the young intern. Not because of what she did after hours, because she didn't know about those things. It was the way the college student pranced around the office and flirted so openly with their boss. The secretary had no respect for her at all. She didn't bother to greet her when she walked in either. Instead she began barking a list of tasks that needed completing.

"Well hello to you, too," Kalia said snidely.

"Dr. Sutton had a meeting and it's time for my lunch break. I'll see you in an hour." Without acknowledging anything the young woman said, the secretary grabbed her purse and left the office.

"Ugh I can't stand that old biddy," she mumbled. Despite how she felt about the woman, she did what she was told. There was correspondence that needed to be typed, invoices to mail and forms to file. She stayed so busy that time got away from her. Before she knew it, both Lily and Dr. Sutton had returned to the office.

"Lily, will you please take these deposits to the bank? I forgot to do it while I was out."

The secretary looked at the clock. "Certainly, Sir. But if I lea-"

"I realize its late afternoon and traffic will be a nightmare," he interrupted. "After you make the deposit, you can head home. You've done a great job today as always," he added, pacifying her.

"Why, thank you, Sir. I'll see you bright and early Monday morning. Have a great weekend."

"You, too." He waited until she was gone to continue. "Kalia, lock the office and come with me."

"Where are we going?"

"I'm making a house-call. Only not to a house."

Kalia made sure the doors were locked and the alarm was set and she followed the doctor down the hallway to the elevators. Although, he owned the entire ten-story building, he leased several of the office suites to other professionals. His office encompassed the entire tenth floor. They took the elevator to the eighth floor and walked towards the west end of the building.

"A gynecologist?" She asked, pointing to the door.

"Yes, this is a gynecology office but it's not occupied now. The doctor who leased this space accepted a position in London. We're here to meet another client. He had a special request. They entered the office suite and Dr. Sutton locked the door behind him.

"Through there," he pointed.

A pretty woman in a white lab coat walked towards them holding a dressing gown.

"Here, put this on with the opening to the front and meet me in exam room one."

To stunned to move, Kalia looked at Dr. Sutton curiously.

"Is that a…was she a…man?" She asked incredulously.

"Yes. Don't dawdle. Time is money."

She hurriedly undressed and put on the hospital gown as instructed and met both Dr. Sutton and the stranger in the exam room.

"Kalia, I would like to introduce you to Nelson Franklin. He's a longtime friend and colleague. Nelson, Kalia Hudson. My star pupil."

"It's a pleasure," the man said, shaking her hand firmly.

"Same here." She was still confused and didn't want to say too much. The last thing she wanted to do was to talk out of turn and offend either of the men. It was obvious that Nelson Franklin was a man of means because he was sporting a two-thousand-dollar pair of Alexander McQueen's.

"Nelson suffers from one of the clinically recognized paraphilias. Do you remember what that is, Lia?"

"Yes, a paraphilia is a condition that that is characterized by abnormal sexual desires."

"Correct."

"While he's questioning you, will you please get up on the exam table and put your feet in the stirrups?" Nelson asked.

"Absolutely." Kalia felt vulnerable being exposed the way she was. Nelson sat in the rolling chair and positioned himself directly in front of her.

"Spread your knees apart, please." When she did, he leaned in and sniffed her center, following it up with a slow lick. "Nice."

Dr. Sutton continued. "His condition is listed as transvestic fetishism. He gets aroused by dressing and acting as the opposite sex."

"Yes, I do. Right now, I'm your female gynecologist. Consider me a lesbian." The two men chuckled.

"The DSM-IV classifies paraphilias as an Axis-II disorder."

"What's the DSM?" Nelson asked while fingering Kalia with his gloved hand.

"It's the Diagnostic and Statistical Manual of Mental Disorders. The four means fourth edition. "

"Oh, so you guys have a big book of boo-boo's for real?"

"Okay, Doc McStuffins and yes we do."

Kalia looked on speechless. The two men were carrying on a conversation as if she wasn't laid out on a table with her legs wide open, being fingered by a man dressed as a woman. They weren't paying attention to her but she was cognizant of this client. His hands were big with long, thick fingers and they felt good inside her. Nelson curled his finger up inside her as if it was making a 'come here' gesture and he began massaging her g-spot. A low moan escaped past her lips.

"Oh, she's getting ready. Let me leave the two of you alone now. I have paperwork to finish at the office. Kalia, meet me back in the office when you're done here."

Breathing heavily, she said, "yes, Sir."

Once they were alone, Nelson rolled closer to her vagina and began sucking on her clit. He had her wide open, literally.

"Damn, girl you taste so good," he uttered, diving in head first.

The willing patient writhed in pleasure and slid as far as she could into his mouth without falling off the table. She loved getting her pussy eaten and this was a great perk of this job because it happened often. Tiny pulsating waves began to course through her body. Trickles of creamy fluid ran down her ass and Nelson licked it off her. Pressure was beginning to form in her pelvic area and her thighs began to quake. She was on the verge of release when he pulled back.

"Look at this shit," he said, standing up, revealing the huge bulge poking through the dress material. "I'll be back. This is some pussy I need to truly sink into."

Kalia couldn't believe that he had stopped before she came. She wanted to rub her clit and finish the job herself but Dr. Sutton warned her against doing things like that.

"We don't want to add to any of feelings of inadequacies that a client may have."

Nelson was gone fewer than ten minutes but that was still too long for her. When he reappeared in the doorway, gone was the pretty woman in the long blue silk dress.

"Damn, your ass is fine," she ogled. The client had stripped off the feminine garb, including the make-up and came back one-hundred percent man. He had on a pair of grey sweat pants and no shirt.

"Let me get up in that shit the right way."

He pulled his pants down revealing a stiff, ready dick, positioned himself at her entrance and plunged in.

"Oh, shit," she exclaimed at the size of him. His girth stretched her out and she wasn't ready.

In and out he pumped, stroking her walls, building her back up to peak. Her clit came from under its hood and he rubbed it with the pad of his thumb. Juices began to pour from Kalia. The natural lubricant gave Nelson access to go deeper, further inciting the riotous fire that was beginning to engulf her body. The skilled lover changed up his movement to a slow, circular grind that sent her over the edge. Waves of ecstasy overcame her as she reached for Nelson and pulled him deeper inside.

"Damn, baby. You're hitting that shit right there." she yelled.

"I'm about to come. Can I come in this pussy baby?"

"You better," she breathed.

Together the couple came with force. Orgasmic spasms continued in Nelson until he spilled the last of his seed in his young lover.

"You are an amazing lover," Kalia admitted.

"Thank you. Sutton was right."

"About what?"

"He said your pussy was so good I'd rethink this whole dressing like a bitch shit and want to fuck you like a real man."

And in that moment, Kalia realized how Dr. Suttons therapy was working on his clients.

"Well now that you've tasted me, it's only fair that I reciprocate," she said. Kneeling in front of his semi-hard dick.

"Have at it."

The two of them went another couple of rounds before going their separate ways, agreeing to meet up weekly to continue his 'therapy'. Once she finally made it back to Dr. Sutton's office she was tired and ready to leave.

"Did you enjoy Franklin as much as I thought you would?" He asked.

"Of course. You know me and my body so well. Everything about what I like. It doesn't bother you to have me fucking your clients?"

"Why should it? Regardless of what you do with them, I know that you will always be here for me. Don't let anyone come inside you. Only me. Make them wear protection like I taught you."

Kalia kept a fake smile on her face because she had let several of his clients spill their seed inside her. They tipped better when she did and for her, it was all about the money.

"I make sure they're well protected, babe," she lied.

"Good. Now come suck my dick. Thinking about you with N.F. made my dick hard."

Obediently, she made her way to the other side of his desk and kneeled on the floor in front of him.

"Oh, before I forget, here's your fee for this client." He handed her an unsealed envelope. She pulled out a cashier's check for fifteen thousand dollars. Without saying a word, she took him greedily into her mouth, sucked his dick until he came, and then swallowed every bit of semen.

"You're like Maxwell House Coffee, baby. Good till the last drop."

BIRTHDAY SEX

The more Colby found out about Kalia, the more he appreciated her hustle. Funny thing about her was that she really didn't need to do all that. From what he discovered, she came from a stable, middle-class family, with parents who provided a good life for their children. All the Hudson clan was doing great things with their lives. The oldest son, KJ had hoop dreams. Kayla, the oldest daughter was in law school following in her father's footsteps. One twin was marrying well while the other was pursuing a career in the music industry. One thing he didn't understand is why Kalia felt that she was raised in poverty. He walked to his aunt's work room and asked her.

"Monty, why do you think a person who was raised well, would think that their life was bad?" He inquired of his aunt.

"More than likely that person grew up with people who had more than they did. We tend to compare our lives with those who are closest to us and if something in our life doesn't match up to theirs, then that's when we start to complain. But then again, what we see on the outside of someone's life, isn't always what's real."

"You are such a wise old bird," he said, kissing her affectionately on her cheek.

"Hmm, mmm. Call me old one more time and I'll take a strap to your backside."

"Yes, Ma'am. You know I love you girl."

"I love you, too. Now get outta here so I can finish selecting flowers. We have a big event coming up."

Colby left his aunt at her flower shop and went to his car. He used the Bluetooth feature to call Kalia.

"Hello." She sounded groggy.

"Happy birthday, beautiful."

"Thank you, babe."

"Did I wake you?"

"Kinda, but you're good. What's up, wit'cha?"

"Just left Monty. Want to grab lunch somewhere?"

"Wish I could, babe but I'm supposed to be going with those people to help with last minute wedding details?"

"Didn't your sister kick you out of her wedding?"

"Yep, but my mother said I needed to be there to support her anyway. Raincheck?"

"Sure. Get your sleepy butt up and get there so I can have you later, okay?"

"Deal. I love you."

"Okay. Later."

The fact that he hadn't said 'I love you' back didn't escape her attention.

Maybe he didn't hear me.

Kalia shook it off and prepared herself mentally for the day ahead. For the past two weeks, she had met Nelson Franklin every other day. Each meeting was always something different. They never met in the same place and he never fucked her the same way twice either. If he wasn't so old he could be a keeper. Forty-six was almost over the hill even though he looked better than most twenty-one-year old's she knew. His age could be easily overlooked though because Kalia discovered that he was a multi-millionaire and his wealth was growing by leaps and bounds.

Having begun his empire in logistics, he later broadened the scope of his enterprise to include one of Atlanta's largest consulting firms, real-estate development, gas stations, funeral homes, and over seventy-five McDonald's locations across the country. She was going to keep seeing him to see if things

107

developed with him further. Their first encounter was the last time that he dressed and acted like a woman. He was all man. And thanks to those clandestine meetings, her bank account was nearing fifty-thousand dollars. Or rather it would have been close to that point had she not squandered most of it on expensive clothes, shoes and handbags.

"Thank God for small favors." She thought regarding him and his great 'tips'.

After dressing, Kalia drove to her parent's home. It took her a minute to get out of the car because she was dreading going inside.

"Ugh...these motherfuckers," she mumbled out loud.

As she exited the car, her sister, Kelli walked outside, followed by her mother and Kennedi.

"Happy birthday, baby sis."

"Hey, Kels. Thank you. How's it going?" She spoke.

"Is she the only one you see?" Kennedi retorted.

"The only one who matters," Kalia snapped back.

"Dumb, bitch. You're not going to even acknowledge our mother?"

"I didn't even see her standing behind your big-headed ass, Kennedi," she lied. "Hey Mother," she said nonchalantly leaning in to hug her.

"Hello, Kalia," her mother said, rolling her eyes. "Happy Birthday."

"Thanks, Ma. Where are you all going?" She asked.

"To the bridal shop. Where else?"

"You've got one more time to snap at me, Kennedi."

"Or else what, Kalia?"

"Both of you stop it." Their mother reprimanded. "You're too grown to be acting like two-year old's."

"She started it," Kalia whined.

"Spoken like the true baby that you are," Kennedi threw in.

Kalia rolled her eyes and ignored the comment.

"If you all are going there then why did you have me meet you all here? I could have driven to the shop?" She complained.

"Because Kalia, I assumed that if that was an option you may not show up," her mothered answered. "I want to spend time with all of my girls today in honor of my baby's birthday."

"All of us? Where's Kayla then?"

"Right behind you, lil' sis. Happy born day, ladybug."

Kalia turned around and hugged her older sister. Their mother walked to her SUV and they all piled in, headed to the boutique for their dress fittings. It angered Kalia that they would want her to tag-a-long in the first place considering that Kennedi kicked her out of her wedding last month for cussing her out. She was glad about it, honestly. It wasn't like she really wanted to be in the wedding in the first place. Her sister was marrying the man that Kalia fancied herself in love with and to top it all off, she was going to be the very thing that Kalia longed to be her whole life, filthy rich.

Once they arrived at the boutique, they all got out and Kalia looked on, impressed as her mother's Range Rover was valet parked. *All About Her Bridal Boutique* was Atlanta's most exclusive salon that catered to only the wealthiest clientele. Appointments were booked as far in advance as two years. It was Justin's money and reputation that got her sister in as quickly as she had. The security guard greeted them at the door and a young hostess escorted them to their private parlor.

"Mrs. Andell will be with you all shortly. May I offer you all anything to drink?"

"What do you have?" Kennedi asked. "I am a bit thirsty."

"We offer champagne, white wine, tea and soda…Coca-Cola products."

"You all don't have red wine?" Kelli asked curiously.

"No. We don't have any red colored drinks in the boutique at all because all red drinks contain Red Dye-40 and while it's not for certain it's in red wines, that's not a chance we're willing to take here."

"I understand the precaution. If a bride were to spill it on her dress that's she trying on, that could prove to be disastrous," Kelli said, offering insight.

"Indeed. However, it's not the bride we are concerned with," the hostess admitted. "It's her bridal party or entourage that's more likely to "accidentally" spill the drinks. For some reason, even though they are genuinely happy for their friend, there's always at least one in every group who has the slightest tinge of jealousy," she finished.

"What the fuck are you looking at me for?" Kalia popped off.

"Kalia, do not embarrass your sister."

"Her? Why did this trick look at me like I'm the jealous one in the group then?"

Probably because you are, Kennedi thought to herself.

"I assure you, ma'am that I didn't mean to imply anything, I was simply turning to ask your drink preference," the hostess said nervously.

"Mom, please get your daughter. It may be her birthday, but this is *my* time, not hers. We're supposed to be having a good time."

"She's right, Lia. Calm down. This young lady wasn't talking about you. I apologize for my baby sister," Kayla expressed. "She's off her meds today."

The hostess nodded silently, took their drink orders and left the room. The sisters all started in at once on Kalia.

"What in the hell was that about?"

"Are you crazy?"

"Why do you always pull stunts like this?"

They were all talking so fast and at the same time Kalia wasn't sure who asked her what. All she knew was that she wanted to spit in all three of their faces and get the fuck out of that building.

"Quiet, all of you."

The girls hushed immediately.

"Now, I'm not going to say this again. We are here for Kennedi but I want to spend the day with all my girls. But peacefully. Got it?"

"Yes, ma'am," they agreed in unison.

A few moments later a handsome man joined them in the parlor.

"Well if it isn't the future Mrs. J-Way," he said, hugging Kennedi, referring to Justin's nickname that Shaquille O'Neal gave the young man when he entered the basketball league.

"Landry, it's always a pleasure to see you," she said. "Is my dress ready?" she asked excitedly.

"Absolutely. Follow me."

He escorted her to the fitting room and different hostess returned, carrying the tray of beverages for the ladies.

"Humph, looks like your daughter ran the other girl away."

"Fuck her. She was obviously a weakling if one little comment can have her running scared."

No one replied to her. They all rolled their eyes in the tops of their head because they knew if they let it go, she would have no choice but to follow suit.

"Here she is," the man announced, pulling back the long drapery as Kennedi stepped up onto the runway that led to the center of the parlor.

Her mother gasped and her eyes filled with tears.

"What's wrong, Mommy? Don't you like it?" Kennedi inquired.

"Like it? I love it. You are already gorgeous daughter and this dress only serves to enhance your beauty."

"Thank you so much."

The dress was stunning. It was a custom-made Andell Fairytale Wedding Gown. It was a strapless vintage ball gown made of silk and satin with silver and gold embroidery. Dripping with hand beading and detail, the dress was heavy and very luxurious. A full petticoat system and matching hand beaded Cathedral Veil completed the princess look. All the women and the man fawned over the beautiful bride-to-be and her dress. Except Kalia. She sat on the sofa looking on in disgust. Her phone pinged in her purse and she checked her text message.

Da One: Wifey.

Ms. K: Sup, husband?

Da One: I miss you. Wyd?

Ms. K: Imu2. Sitting here in hell.

Da One: Lol. What's going on?

Ms. K: This bitch in here getting on my damned nerves. She got this ugly ass dress on and people act like she's Cinder-fucking-rella.

Da One: Jealous much? And stop cursing. What have I told you about that?

Ms. K: Ok and no I'm not jealous. I don't want to be here. I'm not even in the wedding.

Da One: That's your doing. I'm sure if you ask her nicely, she'll let you back in.

Ms. K: Bump that. I'm cool on her.

Da One: I here you. Take a picture of the dress and let me see it.

Kalia did as she was asked and then sent the picture.

Da One: Dang. That dress is amazing. Is that an Andell Original?

Ms. K: Yeah. So.

Da One: That must have set your parent's back a pretty penny.

Ms. K: Nope. The basketball player is paying for this wedding.

Da One: I would love to see you walking down the aisle towards me in something like that. Ask your sister how much it was.

Ms. K: Nope.

Da One: Come on man.

At that moment, Landry asked "Are you excited about seeing Usher and Fantasia sing at your sister's wedding?"

"Why should I be? They're regular people like you and I," she replied.

Rolling his eyes, he asked, "how do you like the dress?"

"It's amazing," she gushed exaggeratedly, repeating what Colby texted her. "How much does a work of art like this cost?"

"This dress is twenty-two, I believe."

"Hmm, that's not bad. Twenty-two hundred is actually inexpensive for the quality of work that you all put in it."

"*Twenty-two thousand,*" Kennedi corrected.

Nausea set in the young woman's stomach. "That's still not bad," she said, trying to play it off like the price didn't matter. Although she had money saved up, she was hoping to snag a wealthy husband too so she could have all the bells and whistles for her wedding like this one. She dropped her head and returned to texting her man.

Ms. K: This fool said this dress cost 22K

Da One: I can believe that. I'm going to have you decked out in a dress like that. Watch.

Ms. K: Really babe?

Da One: Yes. Only the best for you, Wife. We're still on for dinner tonight?

Ms. K: Of course. Where are we going?

Da One: It's a birthday surprise. Got to go. I'm here at the mission serving food. I'll ttyl.

Ms. K: Ok. I love you.

He didn't text back she noticed but blew it off. For the remainder of the time that she was with her family, she was on her best behavior. As the Hudson women dined in Buckhead, Colby served food in Midtown homeless shelter where he volunteered twice a week.

"Mr. C, how long have you been coming down here helping?" A young transient asked him.

"Almost five years, why?"

"Just wondering. You look to be about my age and have it all together. I could have really been great if I had people to support me. Your parents must be very proud."

"I'm an orphan. My aunt raised me after my dad died and my mom abandoned me."

"Damn, you had it rough like me."

The two men sat and talked and Colby got to know the man better. He found out that the young man, Austin, was indeed his age and that he had been on his own since he was fifteen. During their conversation, Colby came up with an idea.

"I really want to work so that I can change my life," Austin said. "But no one will let me come inside their businesses looking and smelling like this."

"How would you like to come work for my family? My aunt owns a prestigious flower business but she has a warehouse where she stores her flowers and vases and such. She could use a hard worker like you."

"Man, that would be great. But I can't go in there looking like this," he said holding his dirty shirt out in front of him.

"No worries. How would you like to earn some quick cash legally to buy some clothes and have some fun at the same time?"

"What do I have to do?"

Colby leaned over and whispered to his new friend who was intrigued by the wealthy man who had so easily befriended him.

Later that night, after he wined and dined her, Colby escorted Kalia to his hotel room at the luxurious St. Regis Hotel in Buckhead. There were rose petals scattered all over the floor, bed and some floating in the luxurious garden tub but they wouldn't be bathing anytime soon. The soft glow of candle light filled the room.

"This is perfect." She stood on her tip toes and kissed him passionately on the lips.

"Not as perfect as you," he said.

Lightly he trailed kisses down the back of her neck as he unfastened her blouse, caressing her gently. Her shirt fell to the floor, exposing her braless breasts.

"Your nipples are hard like diamonds."

With his tongue, he flicked the right, then left one, teasing her. A tingling sensation began to course through her body. Slowly, he lifted her skirt and slid his fingers between her moist folds that was getting more lubricated with every stroke.

"My dick is so ready to please you. Can you tell?"

He grabbed her hand and guided it to touch the engorged meat between his legs.

"Yes, baby. I'm ready to take you inside of me."

"Soon. First, let me do this."

He spun her around and put a blind fold on her.

A blindfold? This is what he did last time and tried to make me believe nothing happened, she thought but said nothing. The last thing she wanted to do was make him mad. This would be their first time having sex in a long time and she didn't want to ruin it by complaining. One thing she was learning from working with Dr. Sutton was that many people had strange sexual proclivities. Blind folding her must have been his.

After undressing her completely, he led her to the bed and tied her hands and feet to the bed posts with silk scarves. Her legs were spread open, exposing a now dripping wet pussy. His velvety tongue lapped up the aromatic juices that flowed from her.

"Oh baby, yes. That feels so good."

With the tip of his tongue, he made circles around her clit and inserted it into her hole, fucking her with it like it was a small penis. She moaned in delight as he began sucking the hard button. Antsy, she couldn't remain still and began writhing in ecstasy on the bed.

"My god, baby. You're killing me with your tongue. You've never eaten my pussy like this before baby. It – feels – so – good," she panted. "I can't hold it anymore. I'm going to come," she sang. Had her legs not been secured, her thighs would have smothered him. Even as she came, he continued to assault her with his mouth until he was satisfied she couldn't take anymore.

The bed shifted and she heard the familiar ripping of a condom wrapper. Without warning, his steel hard dick stretched out her waiting pussy and began pounding her. He leaned over and sucked her nipples until they were erect again but never relenting with his onslaught on her insides. A small spark of pleasure began to grow, causing a fire within her. He moved up closer, stretching her legs further apart so he could go deeper and increased his rhythm.

Using the pad of his thumb, he rubbed her clit while fingering her with his middle finger and lubing it. Then he eased his finger into her asshole, penetrating her. His fingernail scratched her perineum causing her to wince in pain. He mistook her agony for pleasure. Over and over he rammed her in and out with the finger that had a jagged nail. The more she cried out, the more excited he got.

"Stop, please I can't take it," she whimpered.

He didn't reply nor did he stop delivering the now punishing thrusts to her pussy. He roared with pleasure. Knowing that he was the source of her torment turned him on further. Pulling out of her pussy, he forced his dick inside her sore ass and pummeled her more, rubbing her clit to stimulate her.

All the oxygen seemed to escape the room and Kalia found it hard to breathe as an orgasm began to overtake her. Only the sound of slapping bodies and moans could be heard in the room. They both were sweating, shaking and trembling when they came a few moments later. Colby relaxed, took a short break and then was back inside her. He fucked her like a man who had been deprived of sex for years.

The next morning as they sat at the breakfast table, she had to give him his props.

"You're such a skilled lover, baby. I love how you make me feel. That was the first time I ever had birthday sex. Thank you for the diamond bracelet, also."

"You're welcome. I'm happy that I please you. In every way."

He looked up and saw a well-dressed man enter the dining room. "One moment love, I see someone I need to speak with."

She looked on as her man went to speak with a handsome young professional black man. Her head tilted to the side when she saw him hand him a thin envelope.

"It's obviously not money. The envelope is too small," she speculated.

When he came back to the table a couple of minutes later, she asked him about the meeting.

"Who was that?"

"A courier. He was delivering a get-well soon card to a woman who works at the flower shop."

"Wow, babe. You are such a kind man. What did I ever do to deserve you?"

"It was your mom's fault."

Caught off guard she said, "huh?"

"She created such a wonderful daughter. Thank her for me, later."

He took her hand in his and caressed it. She looked down at his perfectly manicured hands.

"Your nails are manicured. Did you get them done before I woke up this morning?

"Of course not. What nail shop is open at eight in the morning? You know I keep my nails clipped and clean. If I didn't, I'd probably end up scratching the shit out of you when we made love."

Like you did last night. Or did he? She wondered.

LET THE GAMES BEGIN

Since Kalia had been 'working' hard with Dr. Sutton, she hadn't made much effort to spend time with her best friends. Whether she admitted it or not, she missed hanging with her girls. This weekend, she was going to devote her time to them. Colby had already told her that he had plans with his family and Dr. Sutton was going to a medical conference. The only things on her agenda were to drink, dance, fuck, sleep and repeat the whole weekend.

The sun shone brightly through a crack in the heavy draperies that covered Kalia's window. She loved waking up in the beautiful room that the Sutton's allowed her to live in, rent free. There was nothing like living in the lap of luxury. Housekeepers and cooks were at her disposal daily. She never had to lift a finger to do menial chores as she would have had to do in her parents' home.

Of course, the house that she grew up was a small three-thousand square feet shack that was one step away from being condemned in her opinion. What's worse is that it was in a working-class neighborhood. It was practically in the hood. Although it was located on the southwest side like The Sutton's, her childhood home didn't hold a candle to the sprawling ten-thousand square feet structure that she loved calling home nowadays. Every time she drove up the winding driveway, a sense of pride overcame her. One day, she was going to have something exactly like this if not better. And her name was going to be on the deed.

There was a light tap on the door and the knob twisted. The housekeeping staff always knocked and announced themselves like in a hotel. It had to be Riley.

"Hey, you're up," she said walking through the door still wearing her pajamas.

"Yeah, been up for a minute. What you got planned this weekend?"

"Not shit. Are you going out with Colby this weekend?"

"Nah. He has family obligations. I was thinking since Dr. Sutton is away at that conference and my man is MIA, that me, you and Anika can have a girl's weekend. It's been a minute since we've kicked it."

"Sounds great. I know Nika is down too. She was telling me last night that she needed to 'get a life'. Hell, we both do. You seem to be the only one doing anything lately."

"Girl, I don't be doing much. When I'm not working like a Hebrew slave for your dad, I'm chilling with C. My time is not my own, these days."

"True. I never realized that Daddy had so much work in his office for you to do. If this was a paid internship I would have tried to work with him but he said it would have been a conflict of interest."

"Uh, yeah. I don't think you would have wanted to do the mess I'm doing. It's um, boring and time consuming."

"I've seen the stacks of paperwork that used to cover Daddy's desk but it's all organized now. I'm sure it's because you're there to help him. He must really be sticking it to you."

"Every chance he gets," Kalia smirked.

They continued to talk for a while and then went downstairs to have breakfast. After they had eaten, they called Anika who agreed to meet up with them later that afternoon. A few hours later the threesome was walking into Lenox Mall ready to spend some money. On the way up the escalator, Kalia had a sudden urge to use the restroom. When they got off, she told her friends that she would meet them in Bloomingdale's.

"They have a restroom there, Knucklehead," Anika ribbed.

"Girl, it's a bathroom right here. I'll pee on myself trying to hold it. Meet me in the shoe department."

A smile spread across Kalia's face as she walked towards the public restroom. This was one of the places that she and Colby would come to have an afternoon tryst. He loved getting his dick sucked in public. It was something about possibly getting caught that turned him on. As she was about to push open the door to the women's restroom, she saw a pair of shoes that looked familiar, standing behind the partition Colby stood behind when she was giving him head. The shoes were brown leather Gucci sneakers that had embossed G's in them. While Kalia knew that they weren't one of a kind, she did know that Gucci hadn't released them in the market yet and her man was one of the few people to have a pair.

She bent over at her waist to see what was going on. Sure enough, she saw a young lady on her knees in a familiar position. All she could hear was the sexy sound of slurping and soft moans. Instantly she got moist between her legs.

"Take this meat bitch," she heard a man whisper.

Colby? The voice sounded faintly familiar but she really couldn't tell because he was talking so low. Straining to hear better, she stepped a tad bit closer.

"Ah, I love how you suck my dick, bitch."

She still couldn't tell because it was nothing more than an audible whisper also. As tempted as she was to walk around the corner, she was scared. What if it was him? She couldn't fathom seeing the man she loved with another woman. It didn't matter to her that she was fucking around on him. That was business. It was a means to an end for her. She was tired of being poor. But if he was stepping out on her, there would be hell to pay.

"I'm coming," the young man mumbled through clenched teeth.

"Come down my throat baby," the woman said loud and clear.

Kalia was about to step around the corner when two elderly women came into the bathroom.

"Excuse us, dear," one of the women said to her. Busted. The couple scurried to fix their clothes and they left down the hallway in the opposite direction.

"I don't even know why I'm tripping. All I have to do is call him."

One of the older women turned to look at Kalia and shook her head because she thought the young lady was crazy for talking to herself.

"Take a picture you old biddy, it'll last longer," she said as the old lady continued to stare.

Unfazed by the smart remark, the old woman flipped Kalia the bird and walked off. She rolled her eyes in the top of her head and dialed Colby's number. The phone rang three times and he picked up on the fourth ring.

"What's up Lia?" He asked, music blaring in the background.

"Huh? I can't hear you."

"Hold on." He turned the volume down. "I said, what's up?"

"Nothing much. Here at Lenox with the girls. Where you at?"

"Since when did you start questioning me in that tone?"

"Since I saw a nigga in the mall who looked like you, wearing your shoes in your spot getting head, a few minutes ago."

"Kalia," he began softly. "If I must tell you one more time that I am not a nigga and never to address me as such again, I promise on my father's grave you will live to regret it."

"Whatever, Colby. You can check me about calling you a nigga but you won't address the fact that I caught you with some bitch."

"First of all, you didn't catch me doing anything because I'm not even in Atlanta right now. I'm in Huntsville, Alabama with Monty."

"Fuck that. You can tell me anything over the phone. How in the fuck am I supposed to know the truth?"

"You could start by believing in your man the way he does in you. Or do I have a reason not to trust you, like you think you have a reason not to trust me?"

"I'm working when I'm not with you and you know that."

"Oh, is that what they're calling it these days? Hmm, it is the world's oldest profession."

"What the hell are you talking about?" She said, confused.

"Nothing. Hold on."

"Hello, Kalia. This is Monty. How are you?"

Immediately Kalia humbled. She recognized his mother's voice instantly.

"Hello, Mrs. Clark. How are you?"

"I'm fine dear. The next time we come to visit my family, you'll have to come with us. I've been dying to introduce them to my baby's girlfriend. You're the only one he ever talks about."

"It would be my pleasure. I'd love to meet you in person also."

"Yes, dear. Well here's Colby. It was nice chatting with you."

"Same here." She could hear the ruffling of material as the phone changed hands. "Babe I'm sor-.."

"I'll see you when I get back." Click.

Kalia stared down at the phone in her hand. She had screwed up again.

"Fuck." Shaking her head, she hurried, used the bathroom and then rejoined her friends.

"Heffa what took you so long?" Riley asked as she tried on a pair of heels.

"I was on the phone with Colby."

"See I told you. Pay up."

Riley handed Anika a twenty-dollar bill.

"You hoe's placed a bet?"

"Sure did. I told Riley that you were going to use this 'bathroom break' as a reason to call him. He must have cocaine on his dick because you are seriously codependent. Get over it already."

"We had an argument. He's mad at me," she admitted.

"Really? I'm sorry. What happened?"

"I thought I saw him here with another girl and I called him to check him about it."

"Oh, wow. Was it him?"

"No, Nik. It wasn't. He's in Alabama with his mother. I spoke to her on the phone, too."

"Are you cheating on him?"

"Now Riley why would you go and ask some shit like that?" Anika asked angrily.

"Because my dad is a shrink remember and he said that when some people are guilty of something, they tend to accuse their mates of the same things."

"Valid question," Kalia responded like she was the doctor. "No, I'm not cheating on him. I only saw the man's feet. He was wearing those new Gucci shoes and only four people I know have them; Jay-Z, Kanye, the person who designed them in the first place and him."

"Oh, well. It could have been anybody then. But truth be told, there's something about him that doesn't sit well with me. He's too…pretty," Riley said.

"Exactly," Anika agreed snapping her fingers.

Kalia laughed, but she really didn't see anything funny.

Her friend continued, "It's not even his looks per se, it's a particular 'look'. I can't explain it clearly but when I saw him there was something maniacal in his eyes."

"Bitch your ass only saw him a few times while you were sober. You're jealous because he wanted me and not you."

Anika exhaled deeply. "Sadly, I know that's what you really believe. However, you are about as wrong as a person who wears socks with flip-flops. Think what you will but mark my words, dude is *not* what you think he is."

"So, Riley," Kalia began, turning her back without addressing Anika's comment. "How are you and Zachary doing?"

"We're cool. He wanted to get together this weekend but I told him it's girls weekend."

"Who's Zachary? That's not the guy we met at the club when Kalia met Colby is it? I'm so out of the loop."

"Hell no. That dude was nothing but trouble. He was cute and had money and all that but he thought that that was all it took to get me. Money isn't everything."

"Says the girl who was raised with a silver spoon in her mouth," Kalia threw in snidely.

Riley rolled her eyes. "My parent's work hard for everything that they have like yours do. Anyway Anika, I dumped him. He had too much going on. I met Zachary at the school library. He's an architectural engineering major. He's funny, smart and kind. You'll like him."

"Where was I at and how long has this been going on?"

"You were in Jamaica soaking up the sun and its only been a month."

"Okay, soaking up the sun. I was over there teaching. Most of my days were spent inside, remember?"

"Don't' tell us you weren't partying at all?"

"I'd be lying Kalia if I said I didn't but that wasn't my priority."

The friends continued to talk about Jamaica, men and fashion while in the high-end department store. After purchasing a few pairs of shoes, they went on a scavenger hunt through the mall seeking other treasures to buy. The weekend flew by and before Kalia realized, Monday had arrived. Dr. Sutton was still out of town so she planned to lie around and chill.

Unfortunately, the things she had planned for she and her friends were thwarted. Riley ended up catching a case of food poisoning and Anika chose to remain by her side until she was better. There was no dancing, drinking or sex. The one guy Kalia planned to get some from cancelled at the last minute and she ended up staying in watching an A Different World marathon on television. To make matters worse, she hadn't heard from her boyfriend all weekend. All calls and texts went unanswered. This worried her because she felt that he wasn't pleased with her from the last conversation they'd had. Her accusations really pissed him off. And for some strange reason, Anika's words haunted her all weekend long.

"Mark my words, dude is *not* what you think he is."

Maybe she was right. Lately, he had been making snide remarks and comments about her internship that made her feel some type of way. When she would ask him to repeat something he said, he would change the subject. Apparently, she 'thought him up' because as soon as she sat up in bed, her cell phone rang. It was him.

"Hello." She snapped.

"Hey. Meet me at my apartment at noon. Wear a skirt, no panties and *do not* be late."

"What am I...? Hello? Hello? No, this motherfucker didn't hang up in my face." The cellphone was flashing 'call ended'. "Son-of-a-bitch."

It was already almost eleven so she had to hurry to shower and dress. The conversation, if one could call it that, was too short for her to determine his mood. His voice was normal and he didn't sound angry but he was good at concealing his true emotions.

At eleven fifty-eight, she knocked on the door. A beautiful, statuesque young lady answered the door.

"Hmm, she's obedient, C. I like that," she yelled over her shoulder.

Taking a deep breath and exhaling slowly to control the anger that was rising within her, Kalia stepped inside the apartment but didn't see her man. She needed to think before speaking. The last thing she wanted to do was fly off the handle like she did at the restaurant and insult another one of his family members. He was already mad at her, possibly. She didn't need to add more fuel to the fire.

There was a guy sitting casually on the sofa watching television and the girl had sat next to him. They laughed at something that happened on the show. The dude's arm was draped over the pretty girl's shoulder. She released the breath that she didn't even realize she had been holding when she saw that.

Oh, so they're a couple, she mused.

Colby came into view and stood in the threshold of his bedroom door with a towel wrapped around his waist. Beads of water were on his chest. He looked good enough to eat. The mystery woman must have thought the same thing because she got up from the sofa and walked over to him. Kneeling in front of him, she lifted the towel and took his dick in her mouth. She was definitely not a relative.

Before Kalia could get the string of expletives out that formed on her lips, the other guy appeared in front of her and yanked her towards the sofa.

"You know what time it is," he said.

"The fuck I do." She yelled.

"Do what he says or else," her man said. "If you really love me, prove it. Suck my dude's dick. I won't get mad, I promise."

"How is this going to prove that? If you love me you won't want to see me with anyone else, like I don't want that bitch sucking your dick?"

"It'll show that you're loyal to me and that you value what I say. You want to please me, right?"

She nodded.

"Well do this."

Confused, but wanting to show him that she loved him, she did as she was told. The friend was clean-shaven and his skin was very soft. He also had a nice, sweet scent. Strawberries. His dick was only about seven and a half inches but it was very thick. The corners of her mouth were stretched out.

She bobbed on the dick and sucked it as hard as she could. Saliva was running down his dick so she used it to lubricate the length of his hard shaft.

"Spit on it," he instructed.

Again, she did as she was told. While she was on her knees in front of him, she felt her skirt lift from behind. Her first thought was that Colby came to join them. Wrong.

"Damn, your pussy is wet," the girl stated before lying on the floor underneath Kalia. The initial sensation of her velvety tongue caused Kalia to jump a bit. It felt good. Light throbs pulsated in her pussy. She was getting worked up.

"Fuck, ooh," dude moaned. "Suck this shit, boo."

Cold gel ran down her backside and she stopped sucking long enough to see Colby standing behind her with the K-Y Jelly. His dick was slick with lube.

"Don't worry 'bout what he got going on, get back to this dick," the guy said, pulling her hair roughly.

Colby's large hands palmed each ass cheek and spread them apart. Roughly, he thrusted his meat into her and began pounding. The girl under Kalia rubbed his balls as he pumped.

"Ah, shit," he moaned. "You're…so…tight."

Tiny whimpers escaped past her lips. This was all too much for her. Whatever sex she didn't get over the weekend, she was getting now. It was worth the wait. Colby reached his long arm behind him and slid his hand inside the girl. Three of his long fingers moved in and out, in sync with the motion of his dick. He was fucking two women at once.

"Yes, baby. Rub my clit. Make me come," the woman yelled.

"Fuck, I'm finna bust this load," said the dude.

Kalia was also about to come, but her mouth was full and she couldn't tell anyone.

"Lia, take this nut in your ass," her man yelled.

The freaky foursome found their release at the same time. The friend nutted in her mouth but she spit it out and rubbed his dick with it. Colby sat back on his haunches. Sweat was on his brow. The girl moved from up under Kalia and Colby leaned down and kissed her deeply.

"My girl tastes good, huh?"

"You damned right."

"Man, you weren't lying. This bitch knows her way 'round a dick. You've got your very own Super Head."

"Nah, but she is my very own head doctor."

OH BABY

Twenty-one. The coveted age teens can't wait to get to. The legal drinking age in most states. For her, it was the number of people she had fucked or sucked in the three months since Colby told her to meet him at his apartment. He had subsequently introduced her to the seedy underworld of lifestyle groups in Atlanta. Together, they attended parties where he watched her have sex with random strangers. A few weeks ago, they went to a gathering and as soon as they walked in the door a man came up to her and pulled her titty out and began sucking on it.

She knew what to expect and how to behave at these places. Colby had already given her the 4-1-1. Regardless of what he told her to do, she did it. No questions asked. In her mind, the more she obeyed him, the more he would love her. The extravagant gifts he showered her with flowed like water. Every week it was a diamond this or platinum that. About six weeks ago, he gave her cold hard cash after allowing six men, including himself to run a train on her. Now she was pregnant and had no clue who the father was.

Dr. Sutton warned her about getting pregnant. Her internship was too valuable for her to screw up now. For her to graduate, she needed to complete an allotted number of hours. She was halfway there. This couldn't have happened at a more inopportune time.

What's done is done. She had no choice other than to deal with it. Both Riley and Anika told her the other day that they noticed some visible changes in her weight but she blew them off and told them that it was the late-night runs to Taco Bell. There was no way for her to tell them the truth. It was going to be even harder for her to figure out how she was going to break the news to her boyfriend.

This morning when he called, she told him that she needed to talk to him about something important. As a safety precaution, she had him meet her at the Starbucks on Cascade road not too far from the Sutton's. The sex groups weren't the only new things he introduced her to. He had also introduced her to his fist.

Colby started hitting on Kalia for getting slick at the mouth or even for saying things he didn't like. If they were in a public place, he would have no choice but to control himself. As soon as she saw him come inside the coffee shop her heart began to race.

"Hey babe." He kissed her on the cheek. "You look great. How are you?"

"I'm well as can be expected. How are you?"

"Cool. What's up?"

"Um, I uh, needed to talk to you about something important."

"Here? If it's important, you should have come to my place."

"I'm pregnant."

"Really? By who?" He asked with a straight face.

"You, Colby."

"Are you sure, Kalia? As I recall, you've had quite a few dicks in that tight pussy of yours." He laughed. "Hell, I'm still wondering how it stays that tight after the work outs you give it."

"What do you mean am I sure? Of course, I am. I love you. We're going to have a baby. Aren't you happy?"

"To be honest, I always wanted to know what my babies would look like."

"Well, we'll find out in about seven months. I hope he or she has your eyes. You've got the prettiest blue eyes."

"Thanks. They'll have a nice olive complexion, too. An equal mix of the two of us. You'll be able to tell that I'm down with the swirl,' he joked.

"Babe, your mom is black and your dad was white. You *are* the swirl."

"Right. Hey, let's get out of here. I'm supposed to go look at this new warehouse for Monty. She's opening a new location. You want to come with me?"

"Yes. I'm hungry, too."

"What else is new. I'll feed you. Let's go."

He didn't say much on the ride over to the industrial park they went to. She assumed it was because he was thinking about his impending fatherhood.

"We're here." He got out of the car and went around to open her door.

"Thank you. Wow, this is nice," she said admiring the massive brick edifice.

"Wait 'til you see inside."

"Where's the realtor?"

"Probably at home. She gave me the lock box code so we could view it on our own."

"Hey, I like that. We can be alone. I've never had sex in an empty building before."

"Don't threaten me with a good time," he chuckled. "I might have to let Mr. C out."

"Come on then."

She stood beside him while he punched in the code on the lock box that secured to the door. It beeped, signifying he entered the correct combination and then it popped open. Three shiny silver keys were inside and he removed them.

Inside, it was an impressive sight of exposed bricks and duct work, accompanied by polished concrete flooring.

"Your aunt should buy this. I love this already and haven't even seen it all."

"Great minds think alike. She bought it this morning. We close on it in three weeks."

"Looks like we have two things to celebrate."

Twirling her hips, she began to unbutton her blouse. Nimble fingers reached behind her back and she unfastened the bra and removed it. Next came her pants. Lying down on the clothes she took off, she spread her legs and rubbed her pussy.

"I'm wet, baby. Don't you want to dive in?"

"You know it, but first, close your eyes. I got something for you."

"Ooh la-la. Give it to me."

"My pleasure."

The wind was knocked out of her. Her eyes popped open in time to see his foot come crashing down for the second time in her stomach. She tried to catch it but couldn't do that and cover her body at the same time.

"You." Stomp.

"Will." Kick.

"Not." Punch.

"Trap, me you gold-digging bitch."

For each word he spoke, there was an accompanying blow. She screamed but they were alone in the large, empty building. The only sound was her cries and his eerily calm voice.

"Please stop," she pleaded. "I will get an abortion. I'm not trying to trap you. Please."

Silence.

He stomped her until she began to bleed.

"Get dressed. We're going to the hospital."

It seemed to take forever for her to get off the floor. She sobbed uncontrollably.

"Don't cry, baby. I'm here for you," he said softly, walking her to the door. Gently rubbing her back.

Through the tears, she looked at him like he was crazy and tried to pull away from him. His grasp was sure and he kept her near him. Like a gentleman, he opened her car door and drove calmly towards the hospital.

"Ma'am, please help us. My fiancé fell and I think somethings wrong with our baby."

"Oh, no. Don't cry, Sir. We'll do everything we can to help her and the baby."

"Bring me a gurney, stat!"

Another nurse rushed to the car and together, they helped Kalia out of the car and onto the stretcher. They took her pants off and saw blood in the seat.

"We're going to put this gown on you, sweetheart, okay? Let's get this blouse off you."

Kalia was scared that she would have tons of bruises as hard as he kicked and stomped her. Surprisingly, neither nurse said anything about them. A doctor came in shortly thereafter and began the examination.

"At this point, there's nothing we can do. It's in God's hands now."

They gave her a mild sedative and Colby sat next to her bedside. She lost the baby the next morning. The female nursing staff comforted Colby as if he were the one who was pregnant and barely acknowledged Kalia. While she was out having tests ran on her, he left. He came back thirty-minutes later with a dozen red roses.

"Awe, those are beautiful," the charge nurse gushed. "You've got such a caring fiancé."

If only you knew lady, she thought, giving her the side-eye.

Colby handed her the flowers and sat at the top of the bed. Leaning in he whispered.

"I did you a favor and spared you the humiliation of not knowing who your baby's-daddy was." He lifted her hospital gown and looked at her stomach. "Your beautiful mocha skin doesn't bruise it seems. That's good to know for the future."

"What do you- ", she began but stopped speaking when a new doctor walked in.

"Good morning. I'm Doctor Drew. Because you were so early on in your pregnancy, our tests show that your body expelled all the fetus. You don't require any further medical procedures at this time."

"What does that mean? What procedures would I have needed?"

"Well, Mrs. Byron," he began before Colby cut in.

"She's not my wife."

The doctor ignored him but looked upon Kalia sympathetically.

"That means you won't have to have a D and C, dilation and curettage."

"A what?"

"It's a surgical procedure performed after miscarriages.

In a D&C, dilation refers to opening the cervix; curettage refers to removing the contents of the uterus. We do that by scraping the uterine wall with a curette instrument or by vacuum aspiration. It sucks out fetal tissue so you won't get an infection."

"Sounds weird," Colby admitted. "And painful."

"Unfortunately, it's a procedure that I give way too often. This is one of the hardest parts of my job. Witnessing a loss. Do either of you have any questions before I make my rounds?"

"I do. How long do- "

"Two-weeks," the doctor said, interrupting Colby.

"You don't even know the question."

"How long do you all have to wait to have sex, right?"

He laughed. "Right."

"My number one question. Two weeks should be good. That'll give the uterus the proper time to heal. Don't put anything inside you at all. Not tampons or a penis. This will keep risk of infection down. Any other questions?"

Neither had any and the doctor left.

"Well, in two weeks, I'll be back in that ass" he whispered.

The nurse smiled when he kissed Kalia on her temple.

"Ms. Hudson, I have some discharge instructions here for you and a prescription."

"I'll go pull the car around, babe and let you get dressed."

"He's such a doll. You're very lucky to have a man like him."

"Am I?" Kalia said.

"Humph. I'm glad that your fiancé left so I could explain a few things to you in private. Dr. Drew wrote you a prescription for metronidazole. It's an antibiotic used to treat infection. You have trichomoniasis."

"I got what?"

"Trich. An STD. By law you are to notify all your sexual partners so that they can get tested and treated also;" she finished, emphasizing the word all.

137

Angry, but speaking in soft tones, Kalia told her, "I don't know where the fuck you get off coming at me like I'm some whore fucking around on my man. How do you know that he's not the one who burned me?"

The nurse laughed. "I highly doubt that. He doesn't strike me as the type to do that. Since you've been here, he's been by your side. The loss of your child hit him harder than it did you. You don't deserve a man like him."

"Bitch, you better be lucky that we're in this hospital and that I'm in too much pain to fuck you up but let me catch you outside of this place and it's on. Watch your back, hoe."

"You're garbage. Have a nice day," the nurse added sweetly before sauntering off.

Of all the nerve. Kalia had never experienced that level of disrespect before. It infuriated her. When the nurse left, she pulled the curtain so Kalia could dress in private. A few moments later, an orderly came with a wheelchair to take her to the car. When she pulled the curtain back, Kalia saw Colby talking to the nurse. The disrespectful wench was putting her number in his phone.

"Did you get her number?" She asked when they got in the car.

"Of course, I did."

He said it like that's what was supposed to happen.

"After what I went through? What you put me through? You're gonna keep adding insult to injury and talk to bitches in front of me? Wow."

"As I live and breathe I've never met anyone as insolent as you." He turned to face her and pointed his long finger in her face. "The only reason she had my phone was so that she could put the number of a grief counselor in it. She thought that you would want to speak to someone regarding the loss of our baby. You're an ungrateful bitch, lady."

Tears streamed down her face. "I'm not ungrateful. I love you. But you keep acting as if you're innocent in all this. It's your fault this happened."

"No ma'am. It's your fault. Had you not been fucking all of those dudes unprotected, you would not be in this situation."

"B-b-but," she stammered. "You're the one who told me to do it."

"I told you to please me. I never said not to protect yourself. If you would have and then told me about the baby, I wouldn't have doubted that it was mine. However, you chose to let them run up in you raw. This is the price you paid for it. Hell, it could have been worse. You could have gotten a disease."

She was dumbfounded. How had she missed it? Colby was a narcissist. He was notorious for placing blame on her and not on himself. Even when he clearly and most definitely did something wrong, he could not and would not accept responsibility. Her man would not allow something bad to be his fault. It was another manifestation of his supreme self-centeredness as well as a protective mechanism for his fragile ego. The psychology classes she was taking were paying off. In that moment, she was aware that she had chosen an accurate major. Just not the right guy, however. And yet, she wouldn't leave him alone.

In the weeks to follow, Dr. Sutton kept her busy with legitimate paperwork and didn't send her out on any special assignments. Had he tried, she would have had to turn down the assignment, then she'd be in trouble. Unless of course he hooked her up with someone who suffered from hematolagnia. That was a person who had a sexual attraction to blood.

"Hey, lady. Did you have your pap smear today?" Riley inquired.

"Yep. Doc said the coochie is still healthy," she replied.

"Right on. You've been kinda down lately. Everything okay?"

"It's cool. Had a lot on my mind dealing with mid-terms. It's important for me to do well in school."

"You and me both. Want to grab a bite to eat later? Anika's coming over."

"Nah. I'm meeting C for lunch, but thanks though."

"No problem. Are you happy with him?"

"Why wouldn't I be?"

"I don't know. I'm merely asking. Sometimes you look like you're on cloud nine with him and other times you're in the dirt."

"I'dunno what you're seeing but I love him."

"Loving him wasn't the question. Are you happy was the question?"

"Yes, Mother. I'm very happy. Anything else you want to know?"

"Nope. I'm praying for you, Lia and hope that you find what it is that you're looking for." She hugged her friend and left.

"Everybody has something to say about me and my man. They need to mind their own business," she ranted.

The housekeeper came and announced that Colby was downstairs, waiting in the foyer.

"Tell him I'll be right there."

She trotted down the steps ten minutes later.

"Should I have told her to make you hurry up? I've been here for fifteen minutes."

"Sorry, Hun. My mother called and I couldn't get her off the phone," she lied.

"No problem. Where would you like to go for lunch?"

"You want to go to Justin's? I love that place."

"It's closed for remodeling. We passed by there last night."

"Remodeling? The place is beautiful. Why change it."

"Beats me. But since Frank Ski opened his restaurant he's giving Puff a run for his money. People love his place more."

"I've never been there. Is the food good?"

"Excellent. Come on."

Sure enough, the food was everything that Colby said and more. Kalia ordered the fried chicken with sweet potato waffles and it was to die for.

"You made a happy plate," he joked.

"Indeed. Speaking of happy, someone asked me if I was happy with you."

"Really? Who?"

"This broad in my psych class. She said one moment I look happy and the next I don't."

"That's a good question. Are you happy with me?"

"Of course, baby. I love you."

"I love you, too."

"Wait, what did you say?"

"I love you, too. I know that I don't say it often enough but I do. You're my world, Kalia Rae Hudson."

"Awe, baby. I feel the same way."

He leaned in and kissed her passionately on the mouth.

"It's time to go. Big Mr. C is getting hard and needs attention."

"I'm right behind you."

The door of his apartment hadn't closed good before Colby was taking her clothes off.

"You have such a beautiful body. I love the way your skin looks against mine."

Slowly, he planted hot kisses on her body starting from her earlobe to her belly. She was ripe for the picking. Walking her backwards, he led her to his bedroom, stopping when they reached the edge of the bed.

"Tell me you love me again, baby."

"I love you, Kalia. I love you. I love you. I love you."

"Shit, we love you, too," his best friend said, walking in the room.

"What are you doing here? And you, too?" The second guy was the courier she saw at the restaurant a while back.

"They came to help me make you feel good."

"You were doing fine on your own. I want them to leave." She tried to cover her body with her arms.

"We've already seen all that. Stop playing. Let's get this party started right," the courier said, who was actually Austin, the homeless guy Colby helped from the shelter some months ago.

Colby punched her and pushed her down on the bed. "Hold her arms, Mike and I'll hold her legs. Austin, you go first."

Despite her screams and pleas for them to stop, Kalia was raped repeatedly by her boyfriend and his two friends. She was forced to suck one's dick while the other two filled her pussy and ass holes. It was the ultimate humiliation for her. Six weeks later she found herself pregnant again.

This time, Colby took her to a clinic that was in the back of a tire shop. The 'doctor' wore a pair of jeans and a white t-shirt with a giant chronic leaf on the front. The white jacket he put on was stained as was the linen on the bed he told her to lie on. Bags were covered in dust, dirt and grime and a portable oxygen tank had dust on the tank and its gauge. Even the dressing gown she put on smelled. Her legs shook nervously as Colby put them in the stirrups.

"Don't worry lil' mama. Dr. Ice got this all under control. I've done this hundreds of times."

Too scared to speak, she nodded.

"Here, drink this. This shit will numb anything.

She took the glass and drank the toxic alcohol mixture and immediately got a buzz.

"See, told ya. My girl mixed all kinda shit and it's the truth. My patients don't be feeling a muh'fuckin' thang."

The next thing she knew he was poking, prodding and scraping. Then she heard the ungodly whine of a vacuum. She felt every bit of it. When she woke up, she was in a real hospital. Alone. She had been there for two days. Relentlessly she texted and called Colby. Her efforts were in vain. There was only one person she could call who she trusted wouldn't say anything, so she did. It was time for her to leave the hospital and she needed a ride. Next, she called Riley and made up a lie about going away for a few days with Colby. Truth is, she was going to lie low at a hotel and gather her thoughts.

"Thank you for coming to get me. I can always count on you."

"No problem, Shawty. You still gon' suck my dick when we get to the room?"

"Yes, Justin."

No sooner than he nutted in her mouth was he gone. It was the same old cycle. She continued to call Colby until he changed his number. He had moved out of his Buckhead apartment and she no longer saw him around campus. She went to the registrar's office and asked a friend of hers to look him up in the system. The university didn't have a student by the name of Colby Byron. Kalia was perplexed. He had disappeared. Sadly, she realized that he never told her his mother's real name or the name of her business.

One day she sat and reflected on all that had happened in the past year. It was overwhelming. At the end of the day though, she had her friends and although she hated to admit it, her family. Her thoughts returned to something her best friend told her a while ago, *"Mark my words, dude is not what you think he is."* Oh, how right she was.

HERE COMES THE GROOM

Kalia didn't know what it is about weddings, but they put her in a bad mood. The most likely explanation was her many failed relationships. But she swore, they were not her fault. Despite her scheming, blackmailing ways, she believed that one of her ex-beaus would have offered her a trip down the aisle. Colby made her think that they had a future. He told her everything that she wanted to hear and then he bailed on her. It had been six months since he left her and she was only now getting to the point where she could think about him without crying.

Today, she was going to have to put on the fakest smile she could muster and pretend to be happy for her sister. Jealousy ate away at her as she thought about Kennedi. Since Kalia was old enough to remember until now, her sister had gotten everything that she wanted. She was effortlessly intelligent, whereas Kalia had to study night and day to ace a test. Her skin was flawless but Kalia needed a skin care regimen to keep hers looking good. It didn't matter what it was, Kennedi always came out on top. And now, she was going to marry the man of her dreams. Justin wasn't perfect but cherished her sister. Anyone could see that.

Anika and Riley were going to the wedding with her and both were punctual. She got up out of bed and began to prepare because she was slow. A make-up artist was coming to the house to do the girls' faces so that was one thing she didn't have to worry about. They all got their hair done the day before so there was no fussing over that either.

Having been hurt so badly by Colby, Kalia did re-evaluate the way she treated people and made amends with her family. Everyone except Kennedi that is. It was nice to be able to see her dad again and talk to him without one of them getting angry. She was maturing and desired to have the type of familial relationship that both of her friends had with theirs.

Riley burst in her room without knocking.

"Lee, you look amazing. You're going to meet your husband today."

"Thanks, boo. You think so?"

"I know so. I'm so glad that God moved that person out of your life. Now you have room to receive the man He wants you to have."

"Ri, you have been talking about God a lot lately. What's up with that?"

"Nothing. I'm grateful that's all. Do you realize how well we live and how good we have it? When we went to visit my Aunt Mildred in South Carolina, I was floored by how some of those people live. I'm glad that I was born to my parents and that they're the go-getters they are. I can't imagine my life any way other than this one."

"Well, I can tell you how it feels to grow up poor."

"How? You didn't grow up poor."

"Uh, yeah I did. Have you been to my parent's home? It's nothing like this. Look around you. That place is a dilapidated shack compared to this."

"Why do you always do that? What's your preoccupation with money? Since we were little you've always belittled your family. You act like you grew up in Bowen Homes or Techwood. You're an ungrateful bitch and I pray to God that when you have children they don't come out like you."

Ungrateful bitch. That's exactly what Colby called her before he disappeared.

Exhaling she said, "you know what? You're right. My parents did work hard so that we could have the finer things in life. I don't know why I think otherwise. Instead of me going to school to become a shrink, I may need to see one my damned self."

"Talk to, Daddy. You know he'll make time for you. You're like a daughter to him."

I hope he doesn't fuck you the way he did me last night, she wanted to say. Instead she said, "I know. I love your dad. He really gets me."

"Hey, you two. The make-up lady is here. Come on."

"Coming, Nika."

Faces beat and fresh to death they made their way to the church. The ceremony was set to begin in an hour but the church was almost full. Fortunately, they were sitting with the family on the bride's side at the front of the church.

"I can't believe your ass got kicked out of your own sister's wedding."

"And I can't believe that you're cussing in church, Anika."

"Touché'."

Meanwhile, upstairs in the pastor's chamber, located near the entrance of the church, Justin and his friends put the finishing touches on their outfits.

"You okay, Bro?" Dennis, the best man asked.

"Yeah, I guess. I am a little nervous though."

"I understand. I was the same way when I married Angela last year."

"How did you know that you were making the right decision?"

"Funny, I asked my father the same question."

"What did he say?"

"He told me to imagine what my life would be without her in it. I couldn't. That's the woman God created for me."

"Man, that's how I feel about Kennedi. Do you know that I've never had sex with her?"

"Word? How you pull that off?"

The groom smacked his lips, "come on now. I get's plenty of ass but she wanted to wait until we got married. She's a virgin. Tonight, will be the first time for us. Her first time ever and my first time with her."

"She's a good one, Bro. You did good."

They gave one another dap and finished dressing.

Downstairs, Kalia looked over to the groom's side to see who Justin invited.

"Guys, is that Shaquille O'Neal over there?"

"It sure is. This wedding is star-studded. Look, there's Jermaine Dupri. Do you think Janet will come?"

"I seriously doubt that, Nika. Dude isn't that damned important."

"There goes the green-eyed monster. I was waiting for her to show up."

"Whatever. I'm going to the restroom. I'll be back"

Kalia stood and arched her back, poking her breasts out so she could be seen. She sashayed down the aisle slowly, giving everyone the chance to see her. When she got to the front of the church, she saw one of the groomsmen come around the corner.

"What's up, Elijah? You're looking good."

"Thanks, Kalia. You too. Beautiful as always."

"You guys are getting dressed here?" She figured they were at the same hotel that her sister and the bridal party were at.

"Yeah. The fella's are upstairs. I'll holler at you in a few. I need to make a run." He hugged her and walked off.

"Hmm, my Boo is here. I need to see him." She pulled her cell phone out of the clutch purse and sent him a text.

Justin was looking out of the window. Everyone started to arrive, and he was terrified. Soon he would have to meet and greet people, kisses here, handshakes there. He would be like the master of ceremonies without his partner by his side. He talked about the Super bowl with one friend of his – cars with another. His stress level was on ten. Taking deep breaths weren't helping him calm down. He was about to pour himself a stiff drink when his cellphone vibrated in his pocket. A smile spread across his face when he saw the sender.

"This is even better than a drink," he mumbled before reading the text.

Bob: Cold feet? Cold anything? I know how to warm you up.

J-Way: On my wedding day?

Bob: It's just another day 2 me. U down?

J-Way: OMW

Justin sat his phone down and began to adjust his tie. One of his groomsmen walked over and looked down at his phone.

"Dude, who the hell is Bob?"

"Marquis, your ass is nosier than a female."

"Yep. So, who's Bob and why is he trying to warm you up on your wedding day? Furthermore, why are you entertaining it? You on the down-low?"

"Fuck, naw. Nigga you know better than that. I get too much pussy to be gay."

"So, if Bob is a chick, then why do you call her that?"

A sneaky grin formed at the corner of Justin's mouth. "Because that's what she's good at. I'll be back."

"Handle yo' business then, Frat."

There was an empty office that Kalia had found and sent him directions to via text message. She was patiently waiting for him, sitting on a desk with her legs spread.

"You're a handsome groom."

"Thank you."

She dipped her index finger between her wet center. "Want to lick?"

He dipped his head and took her finger into his mouth, sucking the cream off it.

"I can't get wrinkled. Help me out of this tux."

Carefully, she helped him disrobe. Conveniently, there was hanger on the hook over a door in the room and they hung it there.

"My pussy is dripping for you, baby. I need you. Now."

Obliging her, his hands cupped her breasts from outside the material of her dress until her nipples hardened. Quickly he unfastened the buttons and her breasts were freed. She moaned as he took one breast in his mouth and tongued her nipple.

Nimble hands slipped downward and under her dress. His excitement was in overdrive and he didn't even care where he was, only that this woman in front of him was going to be his, very, very quickly.

She stood up as he continued to suck her nipple. Releasing her breast and kissing her again, his hands began to drag her panties down over her hips. She unfastened the buttons at the center of the dress and stepped out of it. He held her back a moment and took in her body. She was curvy in all the right ways. D cup breasts, large on her frame, narrow waist that thickened out to lovely hips and legs that were shapely and not sticks. Her bush was non-existent.

Before sitting in a folding chair, he slipped off his boxer briefs before pulling her closer and separating her legs with his knees. He touched her and found her ready, so he kissed her again and pulled her in to straddle his solid manhood. Their lips locked and with his hands on her waist, she lowered slowly onto him. When she was on her tiptoes barely holding herself up, he was almost halfway inside her. His middle finger penetrated her asshole and she groaned as she sank to the hilt. Up and down she bounced on his dick, using the back of the chair as support.

"Fuck me, baby. Ram that dick in me."

Grabbing her ass, he squeezed the round mounds, slamming her onto him with each thrust. Needing to go deeper, he stood up and she wrapped her legs around his waist. His tongue was playing tag with hers as he pressed her against the wall. He put his arms under her legs and spread them as wide as he could and began to drill her.

"Mmm, baby girl, you feel like heaven," he said. "You're hot, wet and oh so tight."

"Grr, uhn, oh. Damn." she replied, "I'm wetter than I have ever been."

They shortly became incapable of talking and began kissing once again until she started a low pitch moan in his mouth when she began to orgasm. Her body shook and quivered and the pressure inside her became greater and he joined her with hard thrusts of his hips as the pleasure washed over them both. Justin stood braced against her. His arms still locking her in place, they were still connected, kissing one another. Every movement causing a twitch of pleasure that was almost too much to bear.

"It's been too long since we did this," he said, "I hope I didn't disappoint you because this was a quickie."

"No, baby. If anything, you satisfied me," she replied. "But maybe we can try again, and maybe it could be in a bed or on a couch or hell, the back seat of a car."

"Sure, as soon as this marriage business is handled. Gotta go."

"Wait. I forgot to give you something."

"What is it?"

"This."

Kalia dropped to her knees and took him into her mouth. Her tongue circled the soft stick, working it back up to its full potential. Unable to resist, He threw his head back and enjoyed it. She was making love to him with her mouth. Savoring the moment, he allowed himself to be carried away by sheer pleasure. She fingered her pussy while she sucked him off, reigniting the fire within. Drops of cream dripped in her hand.

Careful not to mess up her perfectly coiffed hair, he held onto the sides of her face and guided himself in and out forcefully. The length of him hit her tonsils, causing her to gag a bit. The sound of her in distress incited the riotous orgasm that was building up. Unable to hold back, he came in her mouth. She came on her fingers. Proudly, he looked down at her as she swallowed his babies. Helping her up, he kissed her one last time.

"This is for you," she said, sticking her slippery fingers in his mouth.

"Sweet. Thank you so much. I really have to go."

"I know. Let me help you."

They dressed quickly and tried their best to get back to the way they looked before their clandestine meeting.

"Girl, what have you been doing?" Anika asked rhetorically. Her friend reeked of sex. The least she could have done was spray herself with perfume.

"Um, I had to handle some business."

"You missed Fantasia and Usher. They sang a duet."

"I heard them, Riley. They serenaded me while I uh, serenaded him."

"You are so nasty," Anika giggled.

"Yep."

"What's the hold up now?" Kalia asked, looking around. She saw some people she associated with and waved at them.

"One of the groomsmen is missing in action, I heard. Stuck in traffic or something."

Oh, he was stuck in something alright. He was five minutes late because he was having sex with his future wife's naughty sister.

The organist played softly as the parents of the groom walked in. Her brother Kyle escorted their mother to her seat. The bridesmaids and their handsome escorts came down the aisle next. Then, the chords of the organ began to play Mendelssohn's famous Wedding March. The attendees stood and watch as the beautiful bride glided down the aisle. The flower girl dropped beautiful pink and white rose petals before Kennedi's feet.

Kalia watched Justin watching her sister. She wished that she had someone who looked at her like that. One day she would. Until then, she was going to enjoy fucking her sister's husband right under her nose. He may not ever leave Kennedi but Kalia was aware that he wouldn't stop fucking her either. And she wouldn't stop trying to take him.

Guess we'll both have him, she said inwardly. The preacher began to speak while she was deep in thought.

"Dearly beloved, we are gathered here in the sight of God, and in the presence of family and friends to join together this man and this woman in Holy Matrimony, which is commended of St. Paul to be an honorable estate, instituted of God and therefore is not to be entered into unadvisedly or carelessly, but reverently, joyfully and in the love of God. Into this holy estate these two persons present come now to be joined."

His voice was making Kalia sleepy. Or was it the powerful orgasm she had fewer than twenty minutes ago? Either one, she tried her best to tune him out.

"Who gives this bride to this Groom in marriage?"

"My wife and I do," Kyle Hudson, Sr. said. He took Kennedi's right hand and placed it in her groom's left hand. The proud father kissed his daughter on the cheek then went to sit with his wife.

"I require and charge you both that if either of you know any impediment why you may not be lawfully jointed together in matrimony, you confess it now."

If Justin was a real man like he claimed, then he would tell Kennedi the truth. But that would never happen.

"Be assured that if any persons are jointed together otherwise than as God's Word allows, their marriage is not lawful." He paused briefly, then read a scripture.

"Love is patient, love is kind. It does not envy, it does not boast, it is not proud. It is not rude, it is not self-seeking, it is not easily angered, it keeps no record of wrongs. Love does not delight in evil but rejoices with the truth. It always protects, always trusts, always hopes, always perseveres. Love never fails. Justin and Kennedi come today desiring to be united in this sacred relationship. Please join hands. The bride and groom have written their own vows."

Kalia wanted to barf at the words that her sister and brother-in-law spoke. They were syrupy sweet. Kennedi may have meant hers and maybe Justin meant his too, but Kalia didn't take anything that he said to heart. Especially considering that he was knee deep in her pussy before the ceremony.

"I love you Kennedi and no other woman can compare to you."

Kalia rolled her eyes in the top of her head.

"For as much as Justin and Kennedi have consented together in holy matrimony and have witnessed the same before God and those present, and have pledged their faithfulness, each to the other, and have declared their love by giving and receiving rings and by joining hands, I now, by the authority committed unto me as a minister and a priest, declare that Justin and Kennedi are husband and wife according to the ordinance of God, in the name of the Father, and of the Son, and of the Holy Spirit. Those Whom God Has joined together, let no one put asunder. You may kiss your bride."

Justin leaned down and kissed his new bride passionately on the mouth.

"I wonder if he brushed his teeth?" Kalia asked. Riley responded.

"I'm sure he did, silly. Why would you ask such an odd thing?"

"Well, he uh, ate right before the ceremony. I was wondering out loud."

What she really wanted to know was did her sister taste the juices of another woman on her new husband's tongue?

"Let's go, boo. Everyone is leaving."

"Hold up, Nik. I need to talk to my brother really quickly."

Fifteen minutes later, they were seated at the reception, awaiting the bride and groom's arrival.

"This is so lame," Kalia complained.

"Hush it. You won't say this when it's your turn to get married," her mother admonished.

"You're absolutely right. Let me enjoy this time for my sister," she said faking sentiment. Her mother couldn't tell the difference and if she did, she didn't say anything. The happy couple arrived, did their first dance and then the father and bride did their dance. After the formalities were dispensed of, the party was underway. Kennedi made her way around the room greeting each guest and taking pictures with those who asked. Neither she nor Justin changed clothes after the wedding. They opted to remain in full wedding garb.

"Shit, the dress cost so much you're going to wear it at breakfast in the morning, too," he had joked.

Finally, Kennedi was at Kalia's table and she was hugging and taking pictures with her sister's friends.

"Aren't you going to give me a hug, baby sis? We did it. Can you believe it? I've been dating the same guy since I was fifteen years old and today, we jumped the broom."

Grudgingly, Kalia hugged her sister.

"Take a good look, bitch. This is what real love and a happy relationship looks like," Kennedi whispered in her ear before strolling off.

"Bitch."

Kalia was angry as hell. Kennedi always managed to one-up her in some way. A guy who Kalia recognized from the new NBA Sprite commercial walked over and asked her to dance.

"Why not?" She said.

"I say that all the time," the NBA player told her.

They danced the next six songs in a row. She was having the best time.

"Hey, how would you like to hang out with an intelligent man who respects you, mind, body and soul?"

"Why not? I would enjoy spending some time with an intelligent man who isn't constantly groping me." she said with a laugh.

Maybe weddings weren't so bad after all.

WORK STUDY

"**O**oh, yes baby. I love the way you lick this pussy. Yes. Right there. Don't stop. I'm cum-ming," she sang.

As soon as she came, her lover crawled between her thighs and entered her in one swift motion. He took his time, easing in and out. The hook in his dick guaranteed that he would hit the G-spot and she would come again. And again. And again. She also tightened her vaginal muscles to grip his dick.

"Shit. I love it when you do that. You're trying to make me cum. Take-this-dick-Ka-li-a. Ah, I'm about to cum."

Sure enough, he released the hot cream inside her.

"Let me see you push it out," he said.

She opened her legs, took her fingers and spread her nether lips apart and used her muscles to push the cum out of her pussy. He watched in fascination as it ran out and flowed down the crack of her ass.

"That drives me wild when you do that," he said, rolling over and pulling her on top of him.

It felt so good to be lying in Dr. Sutton's arms again. Kalia loved the hard fucking that she got at times but she missed the gentle and tender way, her older lover had about him. His loving was soft and warm and tender. The kind that she needed when she wanted to feel like she was the love of a man's life.

"I should have taken a Viagra then we'd still be going at it."

"Babe, you don't need the little blue pill. You can go long and strong on your own."

He kissed her forehead. "Thanks. It's been a minute since we've done this. How are you holding up after your break-up?"

"I'm actually over that. I took your advice and gave myself some time to heal and reflect. Some things don't work out and it's nobody's fault. Colby wasn't the man for me."

"No, he wasn't. There's a young man out there who will value you and treat you like the prize you are."

"Hopefully."

"It is. So, I hadn't given you any special assignments because I needed you to concentrate on your book work. There's a lot that you need to know to make it successfully in this field."

"You got that right. Who knew there were so many mental diagnoses? I grew up thinking that there was only bipolar disorder, ADHD and schizophrenia," she exhaled. "I was mistaken."

"While it is a lot to take in, you will not know everything the moment you graduate. This is partly the reason that you select a specialty in the field. It narrows the amount of course work you have."

"Doctor, you offer such wonderful insight." She propped herself up on her elbow. "This will cut down on study time and everything."

He laughed. "In a way, I guess it does. However; we must continuously educate ourselves because things are ever changing. You never want to get in the place where you stop learning and become unteachable. That's many people's downfall in life."

"That's not me. I don't think I know everything." The lies she told.

"Also, understand that although you are using a hands-on approach to treatment, you have to listen to your clients. Don't ever assume that you know what they need until you've had the chance to speak to them in-depth first. Misdiagnosis comes with a high price to pay."

"I hear you."

"Do you?" He asked seriously.

"Yes, Sir."

He nodded his approval. "Good. There's a lot to this business and I want to ensure that I'm helping you receive the best education possible."

"Oh, you are teaching me things books never could. What made you choose this field?"

"I've always liked listening to people and their issues. Because I used to think that I knew it all, I figured what better way to make a living than to tell people what to do and how to do it. And I love sex."

"Wow. That sounds exactly like me. When I was younger, all my friends came to me with their problems. Some even said that I would make a great shrink one day. And I love sex, also. Can't you tell?"

"But believe it or not," he laughed. "People still don't like to talk about sex."

She started singing. "Let's talk about sex, baby. Let's talk about you and me. Let's talk about all the good things and the bad things that may be. Let's talk about sex. Let's talk about sex."

"Exactly. I've carved out my own niche in psychiatry and now I have one of the three leading practices in the world."

"Who have the other two I wonder?"

"Mason Adams and Hope Lee."

"Really? How do you know that?"

"They're my best friends. When we were in college, we had our own special 'clique' and we were paid handsomely for our expertise. All of us were already headed to medical school, we switched some things up in the ninth hour."

"Looks like it paid off."

"Absolutely."

"When I grow up, Dr. Sutton, I want to be like you."

"When you grow up, Kalia Hudson, I want you to be better than me. By far young lady, you have been one of my best students. I see you going far in this field. Pay attention and remain discreet."

"Gotcha. What's some of the strangest cases you've had so far?"

He blew out a breath. "Pheww, that's a lot. I once had to treat a person who suffered from Aqua philia. He got aroused by water. Poor guy couldn't bathe without getting a hard on."

"Yikes. Even the rain turned him on?"

"Yes."

"How did you treat him?"

"Generally, treatment is not sought unless the condition becomes problematic for the person in some way and they feel compelled to address their condition. Most people simply learn to accept their issue and manage to achieve gratification in an appropriate manner. For him, we did aggressive psychotherapy and I had to prescribe him some mood stabilizers. In addition to orgasmic reconditioning."

"Orgasmic reconditioning? How do you do that?"

"Imagery. I use pictures to strengthen appropriate patterns of sexual arousal by pairing it with the pleasurable sensations of masturbation. Basically, before he's getting ready to come as he's watching whatever water source is turning him on, I introduce a picture that will help him switch fantasies at the moment of orgasm to try to condition him to become excited by more conventional fantasies."

"And that works?"

"Most of the time, yes. Those are the same techniques used for pedophiles and many others with mental sexual dysfunctions that have led to criminal activity."

"Interesting. What's another one?"

"Well, let's see," he rubbed his chin in deep thought. "One of my favorites was dealing with a man diagnosed with Klismaphilia. His sexual pleasure derived from receiving enemas."

"Gross. How did you treat that?"

"His issue wasn't with the results of the enema. He wasn't trying to defecate. The issue was he liked the feeling of the insertion."

"Sounds like he was gay."

"He was. Unfortunately, his parents were religious and he couldn't tell them about his sexual orientation. So, to hide it, he would tell his mother that he was constipated and she would buy him enemas. She changed his diet and everything. I was the second doctor they took him too. He was misdiagnosed by the first one."

"Ah, that's why you told me to make sure I talk to them first. I get it now."

"Yes. Had the first doctor spoken to him in depth, he would have ascertained that fact."

"Thank God for doctors like you then."

"Yes. He was one step away from being placed on psychotropic medications."

"That would have been bad for him. How old was he?"

"The subject was a teen so the drugs would have done him more harm than good in the long run."

"Speaking of your special assignments, do you have anything for me?"

"I do. The subject hasn't been diagnosed with anything major; simple fetishism. He's a splosher."

"A what?" The Diagnostic and Statistical Manual didn't mention anything that sounded remotely like this. "I know I haven't learned everything but I don't think I've seen that term in the DSM. Is it listed in an older version?"

"No. A splosher is a person who has the fetish of smearing extreme amounts of food on themselves or their mate during sex. That's how he gets aroused."

"Hell naw. What will they think of next?"

"Don't fret. His inclination is towards whipped cream. The subject is married but his wife won't allow him within ten yards of her with any food product."

"How much is he willing to pay?"

"Per session his rate is ten-thousand dollars. You will get four thousand dollars from that." Dr. Sutton was something like a pimp.

She sat up quickly and the sheet fell from over her breast. "Wait, what? Ten-grand for some whipped cream? There must be more to it than that. What is it that you're not telling me?"

"That's everything. The client desires a beautiful woman who will allow him to have sex with her in any way, using a ridiculous amount of whipped cream."

"How long have you had him as a client?"

"Over fifteen years now."

"Oh, so he's older? What did you do before I came along?" There was a hint of cockiness in her voice.

"Kalia, never think of yourself more highly than you should. You are not the first intern who I've been able to use and you won't be the last. I have helped many a career get started because of my knowledge and unique treatment approach."

"What do you mean? I don't think too highly of myself." She was offended and growing angry.

"Yes, you do. The tone in your voice said it. As hard as this may be for you to believe, the world is not centered around you. You're an asset to this practice but you are replaceable at any time."

He managed to put her in check and deflate her ego at the same time.

"When do you want me to meet with him?"

"I'll call him and set it something. In the meantime, I have better things to do."

Laying her down, the doctor positioned himself on top and entered her. She was still wet. As punishment, he fucked Kalia hard and quick, coming inside the hot cave but not allowing his young paramour to climax. He got up and showered, leaving her wanting and waiting. If she wanted to have an orgasm, she was going to have to do it herself. The doctor entered the room clean shaven and completely dressed.

"Where are you going?" The pretty intern sat up in bed.

"Only my wife can question me and the last time I checked, you weren't her."

The sharp response caught her off guard.

"Why are you acting like this? Have I done something to you? You don't have to be so mean. I was asking you a simple question."

Exhaling slowly, he replied, "you're right. I apologize. It's my sister. She fell off the wagon. Five years clean and sober and she relapsed. No one knows where she is. To answer your question, I'm on my way to Gainesville to see if she's up there getting high again."

"Oh, baby. I'm sorry to hear that. Is this your sister, Linda? The one who owns the fast food places?"

"Yep. My one and only baby-sister. Don't worry about making up the bed. Housekeeping will be in today. There are some files on my desk in the office that I need you to put away before you leave. I'll text you the information for Garrett. The splosher. See ya' later."

"Bye, Love."

He kissed her on the cheek and left. Kalia threw her legs on the side of the bed and got up. She walked over to the window and looked out. The Atlanta sun was beaming down

163

on all the pedestrians below. Dr. Sutton had the only apartment in his office building. It was the penthouse. Anytime he wanted to have sex with her, it was there. Sometimes they went to hotels but for the most part, this was their love nest.

Reaching for her cellphone, she hit number two on speed dial.

"Hey, what's up?" She asked.

"Not shit. Chillin'. What you doing?"

"Here at the office about to file some papers. I was thinking about you and thought maybe we could get together."

"For what?"

"Come on, Justin. Don't act brand new on me. What else do we get together for?"

She could hear him sucking his teeth.

"Yeah, about that. I ain't fucking with you like that no more. I love Kennedi and I want to be faithful to her."

"Faithful? Nigga y'all been together for as long as I can remember and out of all that time your ass wasn't faithful. Not one mutherfuckin' day."

"Sure, I was. But it doesn't matter about then. All that matters is now."

"We can't fuck now but we could fuck on your wedding day? What changed?"

"I'm married to your sister, man. That's what changed."

"Fuck that bitch. You said yourself that no one pleased you the way I did. Let me please you now."

"My wife is not a bitch. Don't disrespect her again. And as it turns out, my wife is a freak. She was saving it all for me."

"Whatever dude. I know she don't take that dick down her throat the way I do."

"Good-bye, Kalia."

164

"Okay, okay, okay. Don't hang up. I miss you and it's been so long. You told me that you would always be here for me. Was that a lie?"

"I am here for you. But not in that way."

Today wasn't a good day at all. *Ice Cube I'on know what the hell you were talking about,* she mused. First Dr. Sutton and now this nigga. Could it get any worse? A sob caught in her throat.

"But I love you, Justin. Doesn't that count for something?"

"You don't love me, Kalia. You like me a whole lot. Kennedi loves me. She's a good woman. I'm glad that she stuck around while I sowed all these wild oats because now, I'm ready to settle down and be the man she needs me to be. The one she deserves."

"Please, baby. I need you," she purred. That got him every time.

Not today.

"Not gon' happen, Lia."

Angry, she popped off, "what does that bitch have that I don't?"

"Me." Click.

"Ooohhh," she screamed, throwing her phone on the floor.

She grabbed the pillow and began punching it as hard as she could.

"Fuck you, Justin. Fuck you, Kennedi. I hate both of you."

As much as she wanted to started breaking everything in sight, she couldn't. None of it was hers and she doubted that Dr. Sutton would appreciate that.

Hot, angry tears streamed down her face. Out of all the niggas who had come and gone in her life, Justin was the one constant that she could rely on. Yeah, he was with her sister and she was technically his side-chick, or one of them, but he was the closest thing she had to a long-term relationship.

"He'll be back. They always come back," she mumbled to herself. Her cell phone buzzed in her pocket. It was a text from Dr. Sutton giving her the name and address of the client. She was scheduled to meet him at eight o'clock that evening.

"Might as well make some money since I can't do shit else."

Things hadn't been going her way for a while now. It was time for some things to happen in her favor. Before she pulled off, headed to meet the new client, she got a phone call from an unidentified number.

"Hello?" She hesitated.

"Kalia, Nelson Franklin, here. How are you?"

And just like that, her luck was changed.

"Nelson, I'm fine. How are you? I thought you kicked me to the curb."

"Not at all. Business. Listen, I wanted to know if you were free this evening. I have some things I'd like to discuss with you."

"I wish I was. I'm on my way to a study group that begins at eight and attendance is mandatory. It lasts an hour."

"That's fine. I have a conference call to Japan at eight. They're thirteen hours ahead and anal about punctuality."

"Call me whenever you're free. I'll be done no later than nine."

"Will do. Talk soon."

The duration of the ride was spent with her thinking about ways she could milk this cash cow. The possibilities were endless.

A thick combination of chocolate and semen dripped down her chin and landed on her bare breasts. He dipped his head, licking some of the chocolate from the hard nipple. Kalia tilted her head back and closed her eyes, savoring the feeling of his tongue slipping over her heated flesh.

"Kiss me," he commanded.

"Yes, Master."

Kalia cringed inside calling him that, but that's what he instructed her to do when she first arrived. Garrett Lacy was the strangest man she had encountered so far. In addition to being called 'Master', he didn't want her to look him in the eyes.

"I need you to be completely subjected to me while you are with me. Understood?" He told her after she took off her trench coat. She was naked underneath per his instructions.

"Got it."

"What did you say?"

"Yes, Master," she replied, rolling her eyes when he turned his back to her.

He wasn't as handsome as the clients, Dr. Sutton had set her up with before but he was easy on the eyes. His body was lean with muscle and he was tall the way she liked her men. The only thing she didn't like about him was his dominant personality. He reminded her a lot of Colby.

"Lie back."

Once she was in the resting position he took the can of whipped cream and sprayed down the length of her body. Kalia was covered from neck-to-toe. Slowly he made his way down her body, enjoying the sweet taste of the cream and his willing lover. He laid between her legs and his tongue swept over her chocolate and cream covered center. She moaned pleasurably and he did it again, several times licking off all the sweets before plunging into her center, tasting her body syrup.

Garrett sprayed more whipped cream on her to cover all the areas he previously licked. Her face and body were now covered in the sweet, edible foam. Using a strawberry, he dipped it in a bowl of chocolate and drizzled it over the white cream.

"You taste so sweet," he marveled.

Then he took some strawberries and placed them on her body. One on each breast. One on her stomach. One at the opening of her pussy. Finally, he placed two peeled bananas near her breasts and added a cherry to her navel. Kalia was now his very own banana split.

A low rumbling sound formed in his throat as the flavors mingled in his mouth. Chunky fingers slid inside her, stroking her, building the flames of passion higher and higher until the dam burst, causing her juices to flow and cover his fingers and tongue.

"Ooh, Master. Stroke me, baby. Yes."

Moving up her body, he licked and kissed along the way until his hard throbbing, shaft filled her pussy in one stroke. She gasped softly at the fullness as he stayed still for a couple of minutes, allowing her to adjust to the feeling.

Slow gentle moves were soon replaced by faster, deeper strokes, bringing her to the edge. Engorged balls slapped her ass with each thrust. Moments later, he felt her muscles contract around his dick as another powerful orgasm hit.

"You're all the doctor said and more. This is for you," he said when it was over, handing her money.

She accepted the wad of cash without counting it. There would be plenty of time for that later.

"Thank you."

Don't speak unless you're spoken to. Another one of his directives from earlier.

"Shower. Dress. Leave."

And just like that he was gone.

Doing as she was told, and fast, Kalia got the hell up out of his house. Usually, she would ask a client if they wanted to schedule another session but not this time. It didn't matter to her one way or the other if she ever saw him again.

Hungry, she drove to the nearest fast food place and got some food. As she was getting ready to pay at the drive-thru window, her cell phone blared loudly in her lap. Unknown caller. This time, she figured it was Nelson and she answered as sexy as she could.

"Hello," she said breathily.

"Meet me in an hour at the Marriott by the airport. It's lo-"

"I know where it is," she interrupted.

"Somehow, I figured you would. I'll be sitting outside on the patio. Don't be late."

"Why do you call me 'private'?"

"Because some things aren't your business. See you in fifty-nine minutes."

She was not late.

TIME FOR A CHECK-UP

The time had come for Kalia to have her annual well woman examination. This time, she was going to see one of Dr. Sutton's friends. Her previous gynecologist moved to Virginia, leaving her without someone to take care of her most intimate parts. Fortunately for her, she worked for someone who was associated with great people in every field of the medical profession. Nelson told her the last time that they were together that he wanted her to get checked out. Not because either had a disease, but because he wanted to continue to fuck her without a condom on.

"As long as you're fucking me, you will get tested every month and I require proof of a clean bill of health."

"Yes, babe."

So today she was killing two birds with one stone.

Dr. Cain was a longtime friend and colleague of Dr. Suttons. She figured they attended medical school or university together at some point and expected them to be around the same age. Instead, he was a young, handsome doctor who had a private practice located three floors down from where Kalia interned. Before her appointment, she took the time to check up on the new doctor. According to the gossip mill in the building, he was single but dating, no children, not on the down-low and had excellent credit. Exactly the type of man Kalia sought.

Typical for the first visit, she had lots of forms to fill out; medical history, patient information and the HIPAA form guaranteeing that her information would remain private. The plump receptionist took the papers and escorted Kalia to an exam room where she was told a nurse would see her soon. A light tap on the door and then a young lady in Hello Kitty scrubs walked in. She opened a cabinet and got a dressing gown out.

"Put this on with the split in the front. The doctor will need to give you a breast exam."

"Thank you."

Kalia stepped out of the heels that she wore and began to undress. Before she left the house that morning she made sure to shower and shave. There was nothing worse than coming to a coochie doctor with a hot, sweaty, hairy snatch. Once she had the hospital gown on, she stepped onto the footstool and hopped upon the examination table. A hanging rack that had magazines in it was bolted to the wall next to her so she grabbed a Vogue. Down the hall, Dr. Cain was finishing up another exam and began to make his way towards exam room six where his new patient awaited him.

"Good afternoon, I'm Dr. Cain and this is my assistant, Tracy. What brings you in today?" The doctor took note of how incredibly beautiful Kalia was.

"Just a check-up."

"She's a new patient, Doctor. Here's her chart," the nurse said, handing him the clipboard.

"Says here you were one of Dr. Lakes patients. She's one of my most respected colleagues." He looked from the chart to her gorgeous face.

"Yeah, she was great. I'm glad that she got a better opportunity but I hate she left me. I know that sounds selfish."

"Not selfish at all. I'd want someone to miss me if I were to leave, wouldn't you?"

"For sure."

The nurse sucked her teeth to let them know she was still in the room.

"Doctor, this is the last exam of the day. Remember I'm leaving early to take Joey to the orthodontist?"

Basically, she was saying *hurry up with this bitch so I can leave.*

"Totally forgot, thanks for reminding me. If you need to head out, it's fine. Send Julia in. She can help me."

"Julia already left for the day. It's Wednesday. She has class."

"Dang it. Well, you can go ahead and head out. I'll reschedule Ms. Hudson."

"Thank you, Dr. Cain. I'll see you when you reschedule, Ms. Hudson."

The nurse was happy to leave but even happier to know Kalia was getting out of the office.

"Why do I have to reschedule?"

"Most of my patients prefer to have a nurse present during examination. I try to honor that."

"Well I'm not most patients. You're my doctor. I'm your patient. If I couldn't trust you, Dr. Sutton and Dr. Lakes never would have recommended you."

"True. I guess we'll proceed with the exam. I will be announcing things before I do it so that you won't be caught off guard."

"Okay."

After reading everything from her chart that he needed to read, he looked up and saw that her gown was open, exposing her breasts. He sat the chart on the counter and stepped to the exam table. Dr. Cain couldn't help but appreciate the firm, perky mounds. Her nipples were hard which let him know she was experiencing some type of sexual arousal. The nipples looked like fresh picked blackberries. Pushing that thought aside, he cleared his throat and smiled.

172

"Ok, let's begin. Shall we? I'm going to give you a breast exam. Do you perform self-exams at home?"

"Not really. Dr. Lakes gave me a pamphlet on how to do it but she said women under twenty-five don't have to perform them regularly until we reach a certain age."

"In the past, that was correct. However, we are seeing trends in women under the age of twenty-five develop breast cancer at alarming rates. It's important to be in the know. Lift your arm over your shoulder and relax it over your head like so." He helped her position her arm and then began the exam.

He began on the left side, kneading softly, feeling for any abnormal lumps in the breast tissue or surrounding glands. She moaned a little as his hand grazed the hardened flesh of her nipple. It was done accidentally, but hearing her moan out like that sent a wave of pleasure straight to his dick. It was lucky for him that he had on a long lab coat that concealed the stirring of his loins behind it.

Dr. Cain saw a lot of women in his profession but Kalia was the first that got turned on by a breast exam and showed it. Regarding his type of woman, he liked them all. Thin, thick, tall, short, Black, Puerto Rican, or Haitian. Hell, he was even down with the swirl, but there was something about this woman, lying on his table, who gave him such a sexual rush.

"So, are you in school?" He asked. Maybe the light conversation would help keep his mind off sliding his dick inside her.

"Yes. I attend Georgia Tech."

"Impressive," he said, nodding his head. "What is your major?" The boring conversation was working. His dick was getting soft again.

"I'm going to be a head doctor."

The dick sprang back to life.

"A what?" Clearly, he hadn't heard correctly.

"My bad. A shrink. A psychologist."

"Oh, like Dr. Sutton?"

"He's a psychiatrist but yeah, it's almost the same thing."

"Yes. What's the difference between the two?"

"Psychiatrists have to attend medical school as they are medical doctors and they can dispense medications. I won't be able to do that."

"Is the money still the same though?"

"Yeah. It's pretty much the same pay structure. However, I won't deal with clinically diagnosed patients."

He kneaded the right breast, as he had done the left one prior and completed his exam of the soft, fleshy tissue. He stepped back to her chart, jotting down his findings. His dick was swelling by the second. It was pressing against his slacks and he prayed silently that it would return to its normal resting size before the end of the exam. The doctor grabbed a fresh pair of nylon exam gloves from the box on the wall and stepped to the end of the table.

"Place your feet in the stirrups and slide to the end of the table."

She scooted down.

"A tad bit more. Perfect," he said when her bottom reached the edge. "Now relax your knees and open your legs."

Using his foot, he pulled the rolling chair to him and sat down in front of her, adjusting the light of his exam lamp to see better. *Damn this is a pretty pussy*, he thought. *And its aroused and wet. Fuck.* He could tell because of the width and puffiness of her vulva. Her clit peaked through the labia, hard and erect.

"I'm about to begin. You may feel a little bit of pressure. If the pressure becomes too much, take slow, deep breaths."

"Okay," she said, closing her eyes.

His manhood was jumping inside his pants and throbbing against his leg. He'd never been turned on by a patient before and feared that it was the three-month drought he was going through as the reason for his excitement. He lubricated his gloved fingers and inserted two of them inside her vagina. Kalia moaned out loudly, pressing her pussy down against his fingers, causing them to push deeper into her canal. Her muscles clenched around them, sucking at them and drawing them in deeper.

The doctor had closed his eyes and was thoroughly enjoying the feel of her warm pussy against his gloved fingers as they slid further inside her body. He lost all sense of time and space and he was no longer the doctor but a hopeful lover to this woman in his head. When he finally caught himself, and opened his eyes to look at her, she was caressing her breasts and tweaking at her hard nipples. His dick lurched and thumped and Dr. Cain had the desire to touch her in the most unprofessional way. He was about to withdraw his fingers when her eyes popped open.

"I feel something right there, Doc," Kalia whined softly.

"Right where?" He stated, pausing for a moment as she rocked her pelvis on his fingers.

"Back up a little. More towards the top," she said as he pushed his fingers back up inside her towards her cervix, gingerly feeling for what he might have missed the first time inside.

"There." Her eyes closed and she pressed down harder on his fingers. "Ooh, right there. Can you feel that?" She moaned.

There was nothing out of the ordinary inside her.

She continued to play with her breasts and nipples and his dick continued to grow and strain against his trousers. He

175

started to take his fingers out of her super wet cunt when she reached for his forearm and pulled his hand flush to her vulva. He sucked in a deep breath.

"Oh, God," he pleaded. Dr. Cain was in trouble now.

She began to pump his fingers in and out of her pussy. His dick jerked violently and the spasms sent cum shooting all over his boxer briefs inside of his pants. He pressed his free hand against it, trying to get it to stop, but feeling the pulses of it as it emptied itself out in his shorts was more than exciting and wonderfully new to him. He moaned as the last of the spasms released and the thick liquid from his dick oozed down his leg.

"It hurts sometimes, Doctor, but when it's massaged, it feels much better," she purred.

He lost it. All professionalism went straight out the window. Hurriedly, he removed the gloves from his hands and slid his bare fingers inside her. Pumping hard and fast, he stroked until she reached the brink of pleasure. Her eyes rolled and her legs began to twitch as she began to come on his hand. Her muscles contracted and sucked his fingers deeper into her wetness as the orgasm continued.

"Did that make you feel better?" Dr. Cain asked.

"Yes, a little. But what I want and need now, is that hard dick. I've wanted you inside me since you walked into this room."

She didn't have to utter another word. He had the head of his dick positioned at the entrance of her gash in no time. He spread her swollen lips apart with his fingers and pushed the thick head inside of her wet hole.

"God you're so wet and tight," he murmured appreciating both factors.

He banged in and out of her with sudden speed. All her teasing and having him finger her hole for some imaginary pain that she felt, had his dick rock hard. He groped at her breasts, squeezing them hard and tight as his cock drove itself in and out of her with long, deep strokes. The good doctor felt his balls get tighter than they were before and he saw that it wouldn't be long before his volcano erupted.

Stepping up onto the little step that patients used to get on the table, he steadied himself so that he could drive deeper and further into her. This also allowed him to lean over and take one of her tasty nipples into his mouth. As soon as his tongue touched the hardened nub, he wanted to cum but he held off. He pumped her hard and deep for a few more minutes, praying that his nut would hold off, but his balls were tighter than they were before and he felt it wouldn't be long now. He was buried up to his balls in her juicy, wet snatch.

He released her nipple from his mouth with much resistance from his tongue and grabbed onto her legs that were still in the stirrups. He held them wide and pulled her weight to him with each thrust. When the first sensation of ejaculation came over him, he tried to pull out. But Kalia wouldn't have it. She slid closer to him so that he was practically holding her up and she gyrated her pelvis on his dick.

"Fuck. I'm coming," he announced through gritted teeth.

"Come on, baby," she encouraged.

Thick, hot jets of cum traveled up her warm center. The doctor stepped back and Kalia put her hand out, catching the last few squirts of his come on her fingers and she licked it off.

"That shit right there will send a man into overdrive," he said regarding her licking his cum.

Laughing, Kalia said, "is that right? Well, maybe we can do this again and you can watch me swallow your entire dick next time."

"Hell, yeah. I'd like that."

"Great. Tell me when and where and I'm there."

The doctor put his dick back inside his pants and fixed himself. Kalia eased off the exam table and sauntered around the room naked before dressing. She tossed the paper gown into the trash and began to redress. When she lifted her leg to put on her jeans, he could see her still swollen labia.

"You didn't wear any panties?"

"No, I only wear them when I have to. Is that a problem?"

"Not for me it isn't."

The patient slipped on her shirt and fastened her jeans as he jotted down some last-minute notes. He watched her from the corner of his eye drinking in her beauty and sexuality.

"Do you think I should schedule another appointment with you Doc? You know, to check out that pain I've been having a little more thoroughly?"

"Yes, we should. By the way, I'm going to make house calls only for you. You require special, uh, attention. Let's set something up for let's say, next week?"

"Perfect."

His loins hardened in anticipation of seeing her again. She saw the bulge forming in the seat of his pants and smiled.

He shrugged his shoulders apologetically, "I promise you're the only patient who's had this effect on me."

"It's okay. I get it."

Unzipping his pants, she let the monster sized dick spring free. He pulled on it and jerked it as she wrapped her lips around his fat head. With the corners of her mouth stretched out, she bobbed back and forth.

"Jesus," he called out. "This feels so good."

"Mm hmm," she hummed on his dick, not stopping to talk.

She got his dick soaking wet with saliva, licking it hungrily. He moaned his pleasure. The doctor used her saliva to jerk himself off and she sucked the head for him, hard and fast. He pulled and pushed aggressively, pushing himself to the limit.

"Oh, I'm com-ing," he growled.

Kalia grabbed the back of his ass and pulled him into her so that she could drink his sweet cream like she wanted to earlier. The more he came the harder she sucked. As his tool emptied she softened her touch. She learned the hard way that it didn't feel good to a man to keep sucking after he came.

"Whoa. What did you do to me?"

His head was spinning.

"Nothing much. I took care of you the way I know you would have taken care of me."

"Are you single?"

"Unfortunately, yes."

"Why? A woman like you is a gem. You should be tied down and married by now."

"Thank you so much. Guess I'm still single because I haven't met the right one yet. Who knows. Maybe he's closer than I think," she finished, thinking that he would be a good candidate.

"Who knows," he agreed. She helped him clean himself up in the sink and sat down on the exam table. "Wait here a moment, I'll be right back."

"Okay."

She was looking down at her phone when the door opened.

"That was fa-," she began but stopped short.

"Where's Dr. Cain? I thought that you were going to reschedule?"

"He stepped out and there was no need for me to do so. My time is too valuable to show up to appointments and not be seen."

"Humph. It's supposed to be a nurse present at all times," she argued.

"Only if the patient requests it. I was in good hands with Doc."

The door opened again.

"Tracy, what are you doing here?" The doctor was surprised to see her.

"I got over to Joey's school only to find out his dad came to take him to his appointment so I came back to work. I thought that you may need my assistance. Looks like I was right."

"Thanks, but I'm good. The exam is done. Ms. Hudson and I were about to go over some results. You can start straightening up and stocking the other exam rooms, though."

Kalia giggled. The nurse had been dismissed and was not happy.

"Okay, well. Call me if you need me." She left out of the room in a huff.

"Have you fucked her, too?" Kalia asked.

"Tracy? No. Of course not. I'd never cross that professional boundary." As soon as the words came out of his mouth he wished that he could take them back.

"I get it. The only reason I asked is because she's very protective of you. I think she has the hots for you though."

"Now that I can agree with you on. I've caught her staring at me funny at times."

"Wow. So, what you got there?" She inquired about the stack of papers in hands.

"I ran some preliminary tests of your blood work. I was also going over some notes that Dr. Lakes had put in your file. Did you know that you had a perforated uterus?"

"She may have said something like that. But she said that I didn't have any infections."

"And you don't. But this is different. I'm afraid that..," his voice trailed.

"I'm afraid that you may not be able to have kids. I'd have to run some tests but you could be sterile. Without the results, it's not definitive."

It a minute for his words to register.

"Kalia? Did you hear me? I said you may not be able to have children."

"Good. I didn't want any of those bastards anyway."

Shock registered across his face. Not only because of what she said, but the way she said it. She was adamant in her decision. As much as he was digging his new patient, he was beginning to rethink things. She seemed like a woman he would take home to meet his parents but underneath that warm, beautiful exterior, lied a cold piece of work. His last girlfriend was high-maintenance. Lord knows he didn't need another.

"I look forward to your call," she said, heading towards the door.

"Uh, yeah. I'll be calling you about that appointment soon."

After she closed the door he breathed a sigh of relief. He dodged a bullet with her.

Meanwhile, Riley and Anika sat in the waiting area for their friend.

"About time. What took so damned long?" Riley asked.

"This was her first visit, Chica. She had all that paperwork and stuff to fill out."

"You're right. How was the doctor?" Riley wanted to know.

"Better than I ever imagined."

HEADMISTRESS

The association with Dr. Sutton was proving to be more profitable than Kalia ever imagined. She'd met with Garrett, the Splosher, once again and he tipped her heavily like the last time. That wad of cash that he had given her turned out to be over two-thousand dollars. She used that cash to buy a new Givenchy dress that was on sale. Working with Dr. Sutton was not only allowing her to keep up with the Joneses, she was finally able to surpass them.

In addition to working on the special assignments for him, she was now having more one-on-one sessions with Nelson. That man's stamina rivaled that of any twenty-year-old. And she should know because she had been with enough of them. He was long and strong and his girth stretched her to the limit every time. Fortunately, he never entered her dry because if he had, then she would be in big trouble.

Today, both Dr. Sutton and Nelson were meeting with her at his office after-hours. This could only mean one thing. A three-some. She loved those. It was something about having both or all three of her holes, if they had a dildo handy, filled at the same time, that turned her on. Merely thinking about the two men made her cream her panties. She was getting worked up to the point to where she could no longer drive and concentrate on the road.

As a safety precaution, she exited the interstate at Peachtree and Pine and went into the parking garage at Emory Hospital. She circled the lot until she was almost at the top. There were only a few cars there. She parked, turned off the ignition and climbed into the back seat. Reaching into her purse, she grabbed the lipstick sized vibrator. Not one to wear panties unless she had to, Kalia put her feet up on the front seat head rest and fingered herself with her left hand while she used the vibrator with her right one.

"Ooh, yes," she said out loud. Fantasies of Nelson sucking her pussy heated her up. "Mmm, yes baby."

Moaning and gyrating on the seat, she pressed her pussy against the material so that the friction of it would help stimulate her desire. The tiny dildo was trained on her clitoris and it was causing little spasms of pleasure to travel from her toes up her legs. Pressure was building up inside of her but she kept moving the vibrator and pulling her fingers out because she wasn't ready to come yet.

She closed her eyes and pictured Dr. Sutton's big dick ramming her asshole. The damn was about to burst.

"I would really love to help you with that," a deep voice said, through the crack in her window.

Her eyes flew open in alarm and she snatched her legs off the seat.

"Oh my gosh. I'm sorry. I thought I was alone. I got to go," she finished, embarrassed.

"No need to be sorry. Let me help you with that." He unzipped his pants and revealed a fat, hard dick that was ready for her. "I've been watching you since you began. Don't let all of this go to waste," he added, pointing to his small soldier.

Without saying a word, Kalia curled her finger and motioned for him to 'come here'. The door locks popped and the willing stranger climbed into the back seat. He pulled his pants down around his ankles and sat in the seat. Unable to hold off any longer, Kalia sheathed his dick with a condom that she kept handy in her purse and climbed on top of him.

She was looking out of the back window in her Mercedes, bouncing up and down on his dick. His hands grabbed her ass and he pulled her into him roughly. Their bodies were smacking against one another creating a clapping sound that could be heard in the silent garage.

"Uhn, yes. That's it. Fuck this pussy. Give it to me."

"Shit." He grunted, doing everything he could to get in deeper. "Fuck this."

Pushing Kalia off him, he positioned her on her knees. Using his large hands to spread her ass cheeks, he swiftly rammed his dick inside her ass.

"Ahh," he exhaled satisfied.

"Ayeee," she screamed out in pain. She breathed unevenly for a minute as she tried to adjust to him.

He figured he was hurting her but he was too far gone to stop. To help take her mind off the pain, he reached in the floor and picked up the vibrator. While he pumped in and out of her, he fucked her pussy with the toy.

"Oh yeah, baby. That's the stuff right there."

It was feeling so good to her that she had forgotten all about the pain in her ass.

"I'm getting ready to come. Don't stop. Keep it right there," she begged.

"Fu-u-ck," he sang out, finding his own release at the same time.

Panting, the two of them sat in the backseat looking cross-eyed after their powerful orgasms.

"Damn, and to think that I got mad at my boss when he told me that I had to come up here and work on the lighting by myself. Next time he asks me to do something I'm going to do it and not complain. Who knows what I'll find."

"I'm happy that you happened to be near. I was so horny I couldn't concentrate on driving."

"I'm Lamont pretty, lady. What's your name and when can I see you again?" He looked at her hopeful.

"Hey Lamont. My name isn't important and after today, I doubt that you'll see me again. But I really appreciate what you did for me." She began fixing her garments. "I got to go," she said dismissively.

He lifted his hips and pulled up his pants.

"Oh, it's like that? Fuck you then, whorish bitch."

Obviously, he was not used to being rejected.

"Get out of my car you blue-collar nothing. Your big dick is the only thing you have going for yourself, you worthless piece of shit. A woman like me could never seriously entertain the likes of you."

Angry, the man backhanded Kalia and hit her in the nose. Blood spattered on her white blouse. Shocked and scared, he jumped out of the car and ran off.

"Oh, no," she cried.

She leaned her head back and pinched her nose. Using her key fob, she popped the trunk and found a clean shirt. There was a roll of paper towels in there that she used to help stop the blood flow. Once it stopped, she changed shirts and put the soiled one inside the trunk.

"Fucking low-life," she grunted as she made her way out of the garage, driving slowly to see if there was any sign of him but he was long gone. He was a jump-off to her. There was no way that she was going to try to build something with someone like him. There was nothing lower than a blue-collar worker to her. On a good day, he probably earned twenty or twenty-five dollars an hour. That was nowhere near the salary that she was going to earn when she graduated or the one she required her man to have. In Kalia's life, money mattered.

Because Atlanta traffic is prone to be backed up at any given time, Kalia was smart enough to plan for contingencies. Her little pit-stop didn't set her back at all. Arriving at the doctor's office on schedule, she jumped out of her car and hurried to the office. If they wanted a threesome, she was going to have to clean up first.

Quietly, she entered the office. The two men's voices could be heard over soft jazz music. She rounded the corner and went into the lady's restroom. There were baby wipes in the cabinet and she used a few to wipe traces of her juice from her thighs. Prepared for such occasions, she used her travel toothbrush and toothpaste to freshen her breath. After applying some feminine deodorant, she exited the restroom, on the way to the doctor's office.

"Good evening, gentlemen," she greeted them bubbly.

"Kalia," Nelson nodded.

"Good evening," the doctor said. "Come have a seat here," he pointed to his exposed dick.

That was quick she noted. Obediently, she lifted her skirt and slid down his pole. Traces of wetness were still inside her. The doctor ripped the buttons off her shirt and began licking her nipples through her lace bra. They hardened immediately.

"Oh, doctor. You feel so good inside me," she praised.

"Let me in there," Nelson said.

Obligingly, the doctor raised Kalia up and he laid on the plush, carpeted floor. She straddled him. Nelson came up behind her while she was riding the doctor and shoved his hard dick into her ass.

"You nasty whore. I love the way you take this dick up your ass," Nelson belittled.

Unbothered, she kept making circular motions on the doctor's dick. He loved talking shit to her during sex. It made his dick harder.

"Uhn, both of you fuck me so good. Give it to me, daddies. I need it."

Kalia began to play with her clit, rubbing it in sync with their matched thrusts. Pumping hard and fast, they came within seconds of one another. They had only been having sex for ten minutes. It was quick. But it was good. The men righted their clothes and it was business as usual.

Before the doctor began telling her why he called her there in the first place, he walked over to her and hugged her.

"Thank you for always being so willing and available."

"It's my pleasure."

"More like our pleasure," Nelson added.

"The reason we called you here is because Nelson has brought an interesting proposition to me, for you."

Puzzled, she looked at Nelson with eyes that said, "what's up?"

"Nelson has several lovers as I'm sure you're aware?"

Several? She thought. No, she didn't know that. He told her that she was his only one. *Damned liar.*

"Um, no I didn't, but continue." Irritation was beginning to set in. Or was that jealousy?

"It appears that he has managed to do the unthinkable. He found six women who all suffer from Osaphobia."

"What? All of them?" She was flabbergasted.

"Astounding, isn't it?"

"Wow. I never thought I would ever meet a person in real life who was afraid of giving or receiving oral sex. I love it."

"We know you do," Nelson said sharply. "That's why we called you here. So, you can help my women."

"I don't understand." Nor was she trying to. Yes, she was undeniably jealous

"What we're asking you is that since you are so good at giving head, can you teach these women how to do it? Kinda help them over their sexual dysfunction."

"What's in it for me?" She needed to know what her earning potential was from this interaction.

"I will pay you twenty-thousand dollars cash, if you can help them."

New cars, exotic vacations, and yachts flashed before her eyes.

"You two got a deal. When do you all want me to start? Tomorrow? Friday?"

"Right now." Nelson, snapped.

"Now?" This was a big surprise.

"Yes. They are in the teaching room, waiting for you."

"But I do-, I mean how do I-? What makes me qualified to teach this? I'm not a teacher."

"Experience is the best teacher and you have gained a ton of that."

"How am I supposed to teach them how to give head without a partner?"

"That's what I'm here for," Nelson told her.

Neither man waited for her reply. They got up and went into a large room that had chairs positioned in a circle. Six beautiful, professional women sat in the room, talking amongst themselves.

"Hey ladies, your instructor is here. This is Kay. Kay, the ladies."

The women finished their conversation and got quiet.

"Thank you, Nelson. As he said ladies my name is Kay and I'm here to help you all understand the intricacies of performing fellatio and receiving oral pleasure in return. Before we begin, are there any questions?"

The room remained silent.

"Okay, then. Whether you use the technical term fellatio or call it a blow job, going down, giving head, or something else, this is an act that requires a lot of trust and a little bit of knowledge. In this class, we will dispense of all formalities and simply call it giving head. First thing you need to do is make sure that your man is clean. Now we all know most men don't shave their pubes. If it's hairy, it sweats. If it sweats, it smells musty. This goes double for us ladies. One of our biggest hang-ups about letting him go down on us is our fear of odor. If we do a quick drive-by shower, we can ensure that we are fresh."

"Hmm mmm, you got that right."

"Good idea."

"Next thing we need to make sure is that we are comfortable. Nelson can you come over here, please?"

Kalia leaned at the waist in front of him in the center of the circle.

"If I were to stand like this for a long time, my neck would be in bad shape."

"Wait, I can't see," one lady whined.

"Damn, Rena. Move your got damned chair around here. We told your ass this in the beginning. Hard-headed ass," another woman barked.

"Why don't everyone move their chairs out of the circle and I will stand in front, that way everyone can see."

"Very diplomatic," Nelson leaned over and whispered in her ear.

"Now then, I suggest you either sit in a chair that will make you level with your partners dick, lie down in the bed or get a pillow for your knees if you choose to kneel in front of him. Comfort is key here folks. For the both of you. My favorite position is him on his back and crouch in between his legs with me on the floor. Giving head can put you in a major power position, if you like that feeling then go for it."

"Oh, I like to be in control. Yes, I do," said the lady who fussed earlier.

"Sharon, are we going to hear you ad-lib all damned night or can we learn something?"

This was too funny. Appearances mean nothing. Even the best dressed people can be hood, like these women were displaying.

"Bitch don't make me take my wig off."

"No, please don't take your wig off, Sharon. Listen, let's all settle down." Kalia wanted to corral the hostile women before things got out of hand. "Nelson, since these are your women, I'm sure you won't mind getting naked in front of them, do you?" She asked for his ears only.

"Not at all." He began loosening his tie.

"Ladies, give a round of applause to Nelson who has agreed to be our guinea pig."

All the ladies clapped and a couple let out a few whistles and cheers when a naked Nelson stood before them.

"The next step is tease him a bit with your touch. Use your hands to explore his body. Touch his inner thigh. It's almost as sensitive as ours." Kalia demonstrated the things she said to do. "Touch his balls, caress the dick, grab his ass."

Her touches caused his body to react.

"See ladies, how a few light touches can start a fire? This is what you want to happen. But the fun starts now. For every

191

place your hand touched, I want you to follow up with a lick. Stroke the inner thigh with your tongue, like this." She licked up. "Then like this." She licked down. "Even lick his balls."

"Won't our mouths get dry if we do all that licking?"

"Good question and yes it can. I recommend that you hydrate before giving him head and stay away from salty snacks. The wetter the better in this situation. Next, we take him into our mouth. Watch this."

Kalia wet his penis with her saliva and slowly took him into her mouth.

"While he's still a bit soft, slowly guide your lips over his head. Make sure your lips cover your teeth as you slide gently down his shaft as far as you're comfortable."

She showed them the proper way to do it.

"Keep your mouth taut, as the pressure from your lips will feel great as they glide down the penis. Putting him in your mouth before he is fully erect is a good way of getting comfortable with the size of his penis, particularly if he has a big stick. Watch your gagging too. Since none of you have given head before, you probably don't know how to deep throat the dick. Do you all know what that means?"

The lady, Rena, spoke. "Is that when you put the whole thing in your mouth?"

"Yes, it is."

"Well whoopty mutherfuckin' doo. Your ass got some shit right," Sharon said bitterly, clapping her hands.

Kalia looked at Nelson, pleading for help with her eyes.

Picking up on her distress signal, he turned his head and said "Sharon, what is your damned problem? Leave Rena alone. It's not her fault that I left you and went to her. She had a flat tire for God's sake. You act like she had a baby or some shit. One more outburst from you and not only are you out of this class but you're out of my life. Got it."

All she could do was nod.

"As I was saying, you don't want to take in too much at once. Look here."

She bobbed her head up and down, taking in almost a third of his dick. She could deep throat but wanted to give them the basics for right now.

"Is there a way that I cannot gag?" A pretty petite lady asked.

"Yes. But that's for another class. You must master the basics first.

"Okay."

"Next, as your mouth travels up the penis, flatten your tongue so it gives it a nice, wide stroke. Place one hand around the shaft of his penis while you move up and down on the top half of his penis."

She began sucking his dick with vigor. A few of the ladies were getting turned on. Rena opened her legs and began playing with herself. Kalia saw her pussy and imagined what it tasted like. Focus, Lia, she thought.

"When he's ready to nut, keep your movements consistent and firm — don't slack off. Once he starts coming, see him through with a few strokes and then stop. Most men don't want continued stimulation once they've ejaculated. It could get painful for them."

Alternating between firm strokes of her hand and her mouth, Kalia tried to give Nelson the best blow job to date. It was nice and wet and she could feel the exact moment that his orgasm began to erupt. His balls got hard and she tasted the first drop of precum. Suddenly, his volcano erupted, oozing hot, white lava in her mouth. She slurped the last droplets off and wiped her mouth.

"Whether you all choose to swallow or not, the choice is up to you. Are there any questions?" Hands flew up.

"I saw how you took Nelson into your mouth and he has a big dick. I want to know if it's possible to get a dick stuck in my throat."

"No ma'am it's not possible."

"I don't know what's so scary about giving head," Rena said. "I guess I'll try it soon."

"So how does giving head help us get over being scared to receive?"

There's always one in every bunch.

"Getting head is the most pleasurable thing I've experienced since I became sexually active. When you're getting it, all rational thought escapes your mind. Let me demonstrate."

She crawled across the floor on her knees and dived in head first in Rena's pussy. The woman was caught off guard and tried to push her head away but Kalia kept pressing until she made contact.

"Yelp." Rena said. Kalia's velvety tongue began to work its magic.

Nelson, who was still naked, went and began to lick the lady Sharon's pussy and Dr. Sutton, who had been very quiet up until that point was sucking pussy of one woman while getting head from another.

"Oh, Jesus. What's happening to me? Something is happening to me." Rena screamed, her voice trembling.

"Let it happen, baby," Nelson encouraged.

Waves of pleasure overtook her and her vagina gushed creamy cum. An orgy quickly ensued with everyone fucking and sucking on one another. Kalia ended up eating the pussy of every woman there and being fucked again by the men and a couple of women. By the time she made it to the dorm that night she was tired as hell. After she got out of the shower and her head hit the pillow it was lights out.

Kalia could now add 'teacher' to her repertoire because those women learned what to do to please a man and now none of them were scared. She deserved every penny they gave her. She knew exactly how to get a-head.

IS THERE A DOCTOR IN THE HOUSE?

Graduation day was here. Four long, grueling years and the big day had finally arrived. After all she worked for and as ready as she thought she was to finish college, Kalia was on an emotional rollercoaster. She found herself *not* wanting to leave while also excited, and nervous, about what the future held. Nerves were getting the best of her and butterflies fluttered in her stomach. Looking back over the past couple of years, Kalia realized that she had learned more about herself and life than ever imagined possible.

"Baby, you need to hurry up or we'll be late." Her mother said, knocking on the bathroom door.

"What do you mean, *we?* Didn't I tell you that I was driving myself? Me and my friends are going out afterwards. Plus, I must be there two hours before commencement even begins. I know you don't plan to sit in the stands that, long do you? Damn."

"You'd better watch it, young lady."

"Alright, Mom. But you guys go ahead if you want to. I'm right behind you."

She exhaled her frustration. Had Dr. Sutton not suggested she come home and spend the day with her family to prepare for graduation, she would not be here.

"These moments are special for parents, Kalia," Dr. Sutton told her the night before. "You need to allow them the chance to cherish these memories with you. You're the last of the Mohicans."

"I guess so. Things are still a bit tense over there though. The last thing I want is stress and confrontation."

"Look at it this way, when you graduate, you'll be in your own place with Riley and the two of you will be able to do whatever you want."

"Gee, that sounds great," she said sarcastically. "I'm not looking forward to paying bills, honestly."

"With the money you've made so far, you are set for a while."

Shit, if only you knew, she thought. *That money is almost gone.*

Years of rent-free living in some of the most luxurious accommodations Atlanta had to offer was almost over. With graduation came responsibility that Kalia was not ready for. She loved being taken care of. Good-bye housekeeper. Farewell, chef. It was time for her to get her own place because she sure in hell wasn't going to return to her parent's shack.

The house was quiet when she finally came out of the restroom. Everyone had left. Her siblings were all supposed to come to the graduation but the plan was to meet in front of the Georgia World Congress Center on the Northside Drive side. Kyle, Sr. owned a convenience store near the Georgia Dome and when they went there for events, they parked for free behind his store.

"Buying that property was probably one of the wisest things my dad did," she said to her reflection.

Interstate-85 southbound was congested. Everyone and their mamas were out today. Frustrated, Kalia took her cap and placed it on the headrest in her car to make it look like she had a passenger so that she could drive in the HOV lane. She was one mile away from her exit when she saw the flashing red and blue lights of a police car.

She cursed out loud. "Fuck."

Leaning over, she peered in her rearview mirror to see if the officer was a man or woman. It didn't matter if the cop was

197

black or white. If it was a man or a gay woman, she would get out of the ticket. A short, stocky African-American male walked towards her. He was a muscular-looking man who seemed to be in his late twenties or early thirties. His stride was confident and his legs were bowed like he was wearing chaps.

"Motherfucker," she said. It was a highway patrol officer. They were not as easy to handle as city cops.

When he got next to her window, she rolled it down. He leaned over and looked inside her car.

"Really? You put your cap on the seat trying to fool us? Now I've seen it all," he joked good-naturedly.

"I'm so sorry, officer," she said demurely, hanging her head in fake shame. "I don't know how long you've been following me but this SUV kept driving behind me so aggressively that I thought it would be safer to be over here. I only placed my cap there because it was in the window and slid across my dashboard. I didn't want it to fly out the window. My intention was not to fool you."

She was such a skilled liar.

"Where are you headed?"

He licked his lips. Before he got close, she had unzipped her gown and revealed some cleavage. No man was exempt from her feminine wiles. Not even gay ones.

"The Congress Center. I'm graduating from Georgia Tech. Am I under arrest?"

She put her hands out of the window with her wrists together like she was being hand-cuffed. Drama was one of her favorite classes.

"No, little lady. I pulled you over because you were speeding. Were you aware that you were going seventy miles per hour? The speed limit is only fifty-five."

Gasping, her hand flew in front of her mouth. "What? Oh, goodness. I usually don't drive that fast. I've never received a ticket in my life." That part was true.

"Well, hopefully you won't get one today. License and registration please."

Once he got the documents he said, "hang tight. This shouldn't take long."

Impatiently, she tapped her foot on the floor board of the car. The last thing she needed was to be late for the ceremony.

"What in the hell is he back there doing? I know my shit is legit, he needs to hurry up."

As if he heard her, the cruiser door opened and he made his way back to her car.

"Mrs. Hudson," he began.

"It's miss, I'm single."

"Ms. Hudson, your insurance is cancelled and your registration was suspended two weeks ago."

"What? Are you serious?"

"Very. No insurance is a guaranteed way to get your car impounded. As a matter of fact, I'm going to have to call it in now."

And the water works began.

"I paid my insurance, there must be some mistake. Oh my gosh. I'm going to miss my graduation. What will my family say? I can't even call them because my phone is dead and I don't have a car charger. Oh, no."

She put her head in her hands and let the tears flow. In high school and college, she was chosen for the most lead rolls because she could cry on demand.

"Calm down, sweetheart." He reached in and touched her shoulder. She leaned her head on his hand and caressed his fingers.

"Please forgive me. I didn't mean to do that."

"Don't worry about that. Maybe we can help each other out."

"How? I'd do anything," she pleaded desperately.

"What time does your ceremony begin?"

"Two hours. We have a briefing in an hour but I wanted to get there early so I wouldn't get caught in traffic."

"Okay. Meet me here," he said, handing her and address on a slip of paper. "I'm headed there now."

Got him.

"So am I."

It wasn't coincidental that the paper he gave her was yellow. For anyone passing by, it appeared that she had received a ticket. She put her right blinker on to get back into traffic and in ten minutes she was in front of an extended stay hotel, right outside of Atlantic Station. The officer had removed his shirt and only had on a t-shirt and his uniform pants. He had parked his police cruiser around the corner. Instead of walking over to her car, he went straight to the first-floor room, used his key and went in. The door was left cracked so she walked right in.

"Get up against the wall. I have to pat you down to make sure that you don't have any weapons on you."

"Yes, Sir."

Obediently she stood against the wall with her arms stretched over her head and her legs spread wide. The man put his hands on her back and quickly pat her down, then reached around to the front. She heard his breath intake sharply as he touched her full breasts, his hands lingering there for a moment.

"Ms. Hudson, you need to remove this gown. I believe you may be hiding something under it."

Unzipping it slowly, she removed it and lay it down on the chair by the wall. He whistled appreciatively at the form-fitting bodycon dress she wore. The pat search continued and the skilled hands stopped at the top her thigh when he cleared his throat.

"The dress has to come off. So, does the panties. It's strictly business. We've been having cases lately where young women have been hiding objects in their underwear."

"Oh, no. Not me officer. What would I put there?" She feigned innocently.

"Dangerous weapons or illegal drugs. It's only a precaution for us to take by checking."

"I'm clean, Officer."

"I'll be the judge of that," he replied. "This should only take a few moments."

After she removed her dress and panties, she stood before him, naked except for her bra.

"Assume the position," he instructed her and she got back on the wall, spread eagle. He slid a finger between her pussy lips but didn't penetrate her hole. She got moist. The cop felt around a little, briefly rubbing her clit and running his fingers through her slit, gently. Kalia let out a sigh of pleasure.

"Is this uncomfortable for you ma'am? I'm almost finished here."

She didn't answer. She simply shook her head as he moved his hand around more, getting rather close to entering her hole. She gasped a little and pushed her pussy into his hand involuntarily.

"You sure, you're alright? With a reaction like that, I'd think I'm turning you on or something. I'm only doing my job, ma'am. Don't take it personally," he told her, shoving his fingers inside.

She moaned. "No, you're not turning me on," she lied.

He stuck another finger in her and finger-fucked her slowly. She could feel his dick hard up against her ass.

"Are you sure? You're very moist, Kalia?"

She nodded. "I'm sure."

"Do you mind turning around for me? I need a better look. I might be missing something from this angle," he said roughly.

She turned around.

"Hmm, let's see. Spread your legs. Some girls hide things deep inside their vagina."

He kneeled and got so close to her womanhood that she could feel his breath on her.

"Looks, like you lied to me earlier. You're not clean at all. You have something illicit inside you."

Leaning forward, he planted a kiss on her clit, then kissed down her slit until he reached the opening where he inserted his tongue.

"Mr. Officer," she cried in pleasure. It felt too good to hold in. "Don't. You shouldn't."

Looking up at her wickedly he said, "don't? You don't like how good my tongue feels?"

He licked up and down her slit again, making her wetter and flicked his tongue lightly against her clit.

"Yes, I mean. No. Fuck. Yes. I like it, Officer."

The licking and sucking continued. It wouldn't be long until she climaxed with the way he was working his tongue on her. But to her surprise, he abruptly stopped and stood up. He unzipped his pants and pulled out a dick that was much larger than the guys she'd been with before. It was almost eleven inches long and fat as hell.

This nigga got a horse dick for real. As she contemplated this thought in her head, he inserted his condom-covered dick inside her wetness so fast that she was caught off guard and let out a scream.

"Oh, fuck," she cried.

The officer picked her up in his arms and fucked her so hard she could barely handle it. A long, continuous moan was escaping her mouth and she couldn't stop. At least not while he was giving it to her right, filling her up inside.

Her pussy squeezed tightly around his steel rod and she felt she would come soon. He began to thrust deeper and harder, whispering in her ear.

"Do you know how badly I want to hear you come? Come on this dick, baby."

With those words, she cried out in ecstasy.

"Ah, I'm coming officer," she wailed, feeling the contractions of her pussy tightening around his cock as her hips bucked wildly. He held her in place until the spasms subsided and then gently slid out of her.

"Get on your knees." The command was harsh.

She pulled the overloaded condom off and he slid his dick into her mouth, gagging as she tried to swallow as much as she could. Quickly she got it saturated with her spit and began wringing it like a towel. Right as she found her rhythm, spurts of white come flew out, hitting her on the cheeks. She opened her mouth, catching some on her tongue, tasting his ever-so-sweet juice. The few drops that landed on her cheek, he wiped off and fed to her, watching in amazement.

"That was fantastic. Do you like the taste of cop come?" He smiled and winked at her.

"It was delicious. Thank you."

"For what?"

"You fulfilled a fantasy of mine. I've always wanted to be seduced by a cop. Only I imagined that I would get pulled over on a dark, lonely road and we'd end up fucking outside. Sex in public is exhilarating I heard." No, that was something she experienced firsthand.

"We can make that happen. Put your clothes on and get your sweet little ass to the graduation before I take you the station for speeding and driving with suspended registration while being so got damned fucking sexy."

He gave her a stern, but sexy look. Shaking his head, he gave her a hug and watched her walk out. Now he understood how she'd avoided getting a ticket all these years. They would most definitely meet up again.

Proudly, Kalia left the room knowing she had put on an Oscar winning performance. She was aware that her insurance lapsed. The flunky that she used to fuck with, David, had stopped paying it when he caught her with someone else. He had the displeasure of walking in, witnessing her getting her pussy eaten by his sister. It was awkward. It wasn't her fault that his sister gave head better than he did.

Laughing at the memory, she got in her car and made her way to the ceremony. The dean of students was giving a speech about goals or something. She didn't care. All that mattered to her was that she made it on time.

"Where have you been, young lady? We were worried sick about you."

"I got pulled over, Riley but it's all good. He let me off with a warning."

"Pulled over? For what?"

"Speeding. Where is Anika?" She asked, putting an end to the interrogation.

"She's in the ladies' room. I think Aunt Flo paid her a visit."

"Eww, not today, of all days. That sucks. I know she was planning on going to the room with Sam tonight. Guess they're going to have to wait a little longer. Couldn't be me," she finished, referring to her friend's decision to wait to have sex with her new boyfriend. He had to be getting some pussy from somewhere, Kalia believed. He was too damned fine to be waiting on Anika's square ass. He was probably fucking around like Justin was while he waited on her sister.

"Samuel is a perfect gentleman. Strikes me as the type who'd wait for her forever if he had to. He really loves her."

"Love? They've only been going out for a few months."

"True, but they've known one another since they were nine and ten. I think its sweet that they ended up together after all this time."

"You would," Kalia said, smacking her lips in the process.

"One-day Cupid's arrow is going to prick your hard heart and you're going to fall head-over-heels in love with the greatest guy. Watch and see."

Kalia hugged her friend. "And this is one of the reasons why I love you so much. You're so fucking optimistic, Ri."

"Yep. Oh, here's Anika. You good?" She questioned.

"Meh," she replied blandly. "I was looking forward to being with my man tonight but I can't."

"You guys can still go to the hotel," Riley suggested.

"And do what? Cuddle? Fuck that shit, Nik needs some big, hard dick blowing her back out."

205

Riley and Anika laughed.

"Damn, girl your ass is so vulgar."

"Hell, think I don't know it? That's why you all love hanging out with my ratchet ass, Anika. I say and do shit that others wish they could."

The graduation coordinator signaled the grads letting them know it was time to line up. This degree was the culmination of sixteen years of teachers, tests and studying. It would mark the emergence of Dr. Kalia Hudson. Technically, as a psychologist, she wasn't an actual doctor, but not too many people could differentiate between the two fields of study. Furthermore, she already had some business cards and that's what was on them.

"Ugh, why in the hell is she calling me?"

"Who, Lia?"

"My damned mother," she snapped. "Hello. We're lining up now. What do you mean you don't see me? There are over ten-thousand people here, of course you don't. Don't worry about seeing me; listen out for my name. Dinner with all you people? Ugh, I don't know about all that. I told you I have plans. Alright, Mama. I'll think about it."

"Don't stress, Sis. It's almost over," Riley encouraged, leaving to take her place in line alphabetically.

The familiar swell of chords began to reverberate over the building as the band began to play Pomp and Circumstance. They made it. Kalia fingered the golden tassels that hung around her neck, indicating that she was graduating with honors and marched with pride. She was the last of the Hudson clan to graduate college. Despite her love-hate relationship with her parents, they had done well. They had five college graduates.

When it was all over, Kalia walked away with the assurance that she could do anything. The sky wasn't the limit for her. It was only the beginning.

"Congratulations, Cousin. I'm so proud of you."

Kalia stopped dead in her tracks when she saw an Adonis standing next to Anika after commencement. This man was fine with a capital F.

"Is she the only one who graduated today?" She asked, holding her hand out for him to shake. He turned it over and kissed it.

"Apologies, Queen. Congratulations to you as well."

Kalia hit Anika on the butt and nodded towards the guy, giving her a questioning stare.

"Oh, um, Sebastian, this is my bestie, Kalia Hudson. Kalia, my favorite cousin, Sebastian Rochon. We call him Bash, though."

Rochon? Where had she heard that name before?

"Nice to meet you," she said cordially.

"Pleasure's all mine. So, tell me, what is your degree in?"

"I received my Bachelors of Science in Psychology." She preened like a peacock.

"Alright then, Dr. Hudson. Do the damned thing."

"That's the plan."

"Will you be joining us for dinner later? My mom has prepared a feast for Nik. She swears that this is her daughter," he laughed, pointing at his cousin.

"Hush it up. You're probably jealous because Aunty Mi-Mi, loves me more than she does your nappy headed ass."

"Pssh, she feels sorry for you because when your parents first saw you they wanted to place you up for adoption because your head was too big and you were ugly as hell. Ol' Benjamin Button looking ass."

"I see you're trying to step your game up, you welfare version, food stamp getting Christian Keyes want to be ass. You know light skinned niggas ain't in this year, don't you?"

The cousins continued their verbal sparring for a few more minutes. It was funny.

"So, are you down with us or not?" He asked, turning his attention back to Kalia.

"Awe, I wish I could but my family and I are going out to celebrate."

"But I thought you sai-," Anika began.

Kalia pinched her friend's thigh.

"Ouch. Oh, yeah. Right. She's having dinner with her family."

"How about a raincheck?"

"You're on. Listen, take my number and whenever you're ready to redeem it, hit me up."

"Oh, don't worry, I will. This doctor will most definitely make a house call for you."

JACKPOTS AND CASH COWS

Net worth, one-hundred thirty-two million dollars.

"Yes, baby, give it to me."

Global presence in over one hundred countries.

"Uhn, right there."

Total earnings in the last quarter of the fiscal year, sixty-nine million dollars.

"I'm coming, Nelson,' Kalia sang out.

Juices ran down her thigh as the man continued to pummel her vagina. She was extremely stimulated. Usually, he would begin with a round of foreplay but not tonight. This was a quickie session for him. However, she had just finished doing some research when he came to her new home in Midtown Atlanta. Research that got her so excited her pussy got wet.

It had been almost three months since graduation and equally as long since the two of them had gotten together. During that time, Kalia had moved out of the Sutton's home and into her own place. Initially, she and Riley were going to get a spot together but because of her lifestyle, both she and Dr. Sutton thought it best if she lived by herself. As a bonus for coming aboard his staff permanently, he purchased the two-story penthouse with three bedrooms and panoramic views of downtown especially for her. Even better, he deeded the property in her name.

"Are you fucking someone else?" Nelson asked her.

"No one that you don't know about," she replied honestly. "Why?"

"Someone must have been on your mind when I was inside you. I've never felt you that wet in the four-years that we've been fucking around."

"Has it been that long?" She challenged, rubbing her chin.

"Don't change the subject, answer me damn it."

"No, it wasn't a person on my mind. But I was thinking of my one true love."

"And that's?" He asked, stretching the question out.

"Money."

"Hmm. Speaking of which, I'm going out of the country. I don't know when I'll return. One of my factories in India isn't doing so well. I've got to go over there and find out what's going on. I think the CFO is robbing me. I hope that's not the case. For his sake."

"I hate to hear that. Please know that I'll miss you, baby."

He rubbed her stomach. It was flat and toned.

"No baby in there is it?"

Damn, she forgot she lied to him about being pregnant so he could pay for an abortion.

"I took care of it. We can take a pregnancy test or go get an ultrasound. No baby in here."

"Great."

"When are you leaving?"

"Five tomorrow evening."

"That soon, huh? Well since this is your last night with me, how about one for the road?"

"Nothing, doing. I've got things to finalize. See you soon."

He didn't give her a hug or kiss or anything. He simply pulled up his pants, fastened his belt and walked out.

She didn't care. David, was coming over to tune her up. After graduation, she called him and asked if they could meet up. Once he agreed to see her, she realized she had him where she wanted him. He didn't want to leave her in the first place. But when he caught her, his friend was with him and he convinced him to let her go.

"I run this," she boasted to the pillow as she rolled over on it.

Not sure what time he was going to stop by, she went to shower and wash away the remnants of Nelson's sperm. He still didn't like wearing condoms. Even after she got 'pregnant'. Men were so gullible. He really believed her when she told him that the abortion was going to cost five grand.

"The doctor said it's because my blood-type is rare. I'm Rh-negative."

Without batting an eye, he brought the money over to her. That was the last time she saw him until tonight. Now he was going away for lord knows how long and she was going to miss him. Rather, she was going to miss the money he gave her. Every dime counted in the 'Save-Kalia-Fund'.

"Oh, but if I can get you, boo, I won't have to worry about anything," she said to the picture of Sebastian Rochon that she had in her phone. It was really a picture of both he and Anika but she cropped her friend out of the photo earlier when she printed the report that lay before her on the bed.

She had forgotten all about him. Although he was fine and yes, he did resemble Christian Keyes, if a person wasn't talking about money then Kalia wasn't trying to hear it. Every now and again, Anika would tell her that Bash said this or he said that. It took a minute for her to even remember that that was his nickname. Of course, she would send her hello's or what-not but it was more out of obligation than anything else. Coincidentally, thanks to her sister Kennedi, she may have hit the jackpot.

Earlier that day, the record label that Kelli signed her recording contract with, hosted a day party in honor of her sister's debut album going platinum. Kalia went to support her. In addition, she was looking for a new sponsor. Her coffers were getting low. With the bevy of eligible bachelor's milling around the room, she was sure to snag a viable candidate.

The party was in full swing by the time Kennedi and her husband Justin showed up. Kalia's heart skipped a beat when she saw him. Old feelings began to resurface the longer she stared at him. A staff photographer stopped the couple and snapped a few shots of them. People began to mill around him like this was his event.

"Motherfuckers always making shit about them," she said bitterly.

She was still angry that he cut her off. Justin refused to take any more of her calls after the last conversation. He did send her a text telling her to 'fuck-off'. Those were his exact words. Last week, ESPN did a cover story on 'J-Way'. Cameras were all in the house, showing the world, how good he and Kennedi were living. The reporter spoke to him about his relationship with his wife.

"She's the air I breathe, Stephen. Definitely a gift from God. I wouldn't be where I am today if it wasn't for her and my parents. I owe them my life," he expressed emotionally.

Watching him speak to the world about his wife, Kalia felt pangs of jealousy.

"That should be me he's talking about," she said to the television, throwing a pillow at it.

Nevertheless, it wasn't and eventually, she was going to have to do two things. Build a bridge, then get over it.

As if Justin felt her eying him, he looked over to her and winked. She smirked. The crowd around them dissipated and they made their way towards, Kelli, offering her their salutations and congratulations. Admittedly, the album that she put out was good and Kalia was extremely proud of her. Everyone who was anyone in the music industry had come out to support and show her sister some love. Usher, Fantasia, Faith Evans. So many notables had their face in the place. Even Beyonce took the time to skype Kelli a congratulatory message. Shortly after the party began, Kelli had arrived.

"This is what true success looks like, whorish bitch."

Like the snake Kalia perceived her to be, Kennedi slithered up behind her and whispered that in her ear. But when Kalia turned to respond, she was already walking away. Knowing that she'd never hear the end of it from her family if she was to start in on her sister at Kelli's big event, she chilled out. There would be plenty of time to confront her if she chose to.

Being cordial, Kalia walked and stood by her mother, who was having a conversation with Kennedi.

"Your make-up is so beautiful daughter. Is that MAC?" Karen inquired.

"No, ma'am. It's Fit Mi by Amira Rochon," she told her.

Kalia's eyes rounded like saucers.

"Rochon Cosmetics?" She said out loud, not talking to anyone in particular.

"Yes. It's from her new line, Famous Faces."

Like a ton of bricks, it hit her and instantly her memory began to replay a conversation she had heard a few months ago, on graduation day.

"Sebastian, this is my bestie, Kalia Hudson. Kalia, my favorite cousin, Sebastian Rochon. We call him Bash, though."

More importantly she remembered, *"You're jealous because Aunty Mi-Mi, loves me more than she does your nappy headed ass."*

Was Mi-Mi short for Amira? Was Amira Rochon, Sebastian's mother? A devious smile spread across her face.

"Why are you looking like the cat that ate the canary?" Kennedi asked.

Kalia noted that she was being nicer than normal.

"Was I? I'm actually thinking about my new man." *Might as well put that into the universe now,* she thought. From her mouth to God's ears.

"I didn't realize that you were dating anyone, daughter."

"Me either, Sis."

Sis? Did Kennedi call her, Sis? Kalia put the back of her hand on her sister's forehead.

"Are you feeling okay?" This was not the Kennedi she knew. The one she grew up with had something smart to say at every turn. They couldn't be around one another a second without verbally sparring.

"I'm well. Life is too short to be arguing with you every five minutes. I'm sorry about what I said earlier, too. That was out of line."

"Hmm, well hell, apology accepted."

The two sisters hugged.

"Awe, this is what a mother loves to see. Her children making amends."

"You're right, Ma. I love you, Kennedi. Always have. Just didn't like you much," she admitted.

"Same here," the twin shrugged. "It's all good though. We're over it now."

"Did you hear the good news, Kalia?" Their mother looked on expectantly.

"No, Ma'am. What's going on."

Kennedi blushed. "Justin and I are going to have a baby."

A bright light flashed in Kalia's face. She felt light-headed, oxygen deprived. This wasn't real. Yet, it was.

"Con-grats..um, congratulations, Ken," she finally mustered up.

"Thank you. We're very excited. Especially Jussy. It's all he's been able to talk about."

"Wow."

Whatever delusions she had about she and J-Way reconciling and him leaving her sister for her, were dead in the water now. It was over.

"Kennedi, I'm really happy for you. Really. Both you and Justin deserve this and so much more. Blessings to you and your family."

For once in her life, Kalia was honest. She really was happy for her sister and aspired to have the life that her sister had. Hopefully, it wasn't too late for her to call Sebastian and hook-up with him. He gave the impression that he was genuinely interested in her and at that moment, she was interested in him.

Now, here she sat at home, reading the report she had printed from the internet.

"Thank you Google and Wikipedia."

In a matter of minutes, she discovered important facts about Amira Rochon that made her son the ultimate catch for Kalia. She had three sons and made marrying well an art form. In the early nineteen eighties she had created a facial cleanser out of berries that left skin glowing. Someone in Louisiana saw her doing a demonstration at her booth in the local flea market and loved the results. The man happened to be a former executive from Fashion Fair Cosmetics and he helped her repackage, market and launch her very own line of facial products that catered to women of color.

"This woman is bad," she remarked. Picking up her phone, she dialed a number.

"Hello," Anika answered.

"Why are you whispering?"

"I'm in the library. What's up?"

"Do you think Sebastian would mind you giving me his number? I got a new phone." True. "When they uploaded my phonebook some of my contacts were deleted." Lie.

"He wouldn't mind. He asked about you yesterday, too. I'll text it you. I got to go. Love ya."

"Love you, too."

A few seconds later, her phone dinged notifying her of a message. Suddenly, she got nervous.

"Calm down bitch. It's only another dude," she reprimanded herself fully aware that he was not one of the basic Joe's she knew. "Here goes nothing," she said, dialing his number.

"Hello?" His sexy voice was music to her ears.

"Hello. May I please speak to Sebastian?" Her voice shook.

"Speaking. Who's this?"

This nigga didn't lock me in his phone? The nerve, she thought.

"This is Kalia Hudson. We met at the graduation."

"Hey, Queen. How are you? I thought you were cool on a brother like me."

"Why do you say that?"

"Well I did give you my number and you never used it."

"I gave you my number as well. It goes both ways."

"Yeah, but your number changed the following week. Mine didn't."

"Oops. It did, huh? I'm sorry. I don't know if Anika told you but my phone was stolen. When I got a new one, I had the number changed also."

"Sorry to hear that happened to you. You good?"

"Yes, I'm fine."

"Good lawd, yes you are."

Laughing, she continued. "Anyway, the reason I didn't call you was because all my contacts didn't port to this device." That's her story and she was sticking to it. "Anika gave me your number. I hope you don't mind."

"Not at all. Remind me to thank her later."

Once the ice was broken and Kalia got comfortable, she began asking him the questions that mattered to her. Was he married? In a relationship? A baby-daddy? Interested in a particular woman or even a man? They were in the 'A' after all. One never knew.

"It's hard to believe that a man as intelligent and handsome as you aren't dating anyone."

"I never said I wasn't dating. You asked if I was in a relationship."

"Excuse me, then."

He laughed before replying. "I was seeing someone on a consistent basis but I found out she cheated on me so I ended it."

"Sorry to hear that. Did you love her?"

"It's no biggie and no I didn't. We had only been going out a few weeks. No love lost."

"That's good. Wouldn't want to be stepping on someone's toes.

"I'm so rude, were you busy? I can call you back later." Kalia tried to sound sincere.

"Nah, I was just helping my mom with some things from her office."

"Oh. What does your mom do?"

"She owns a cosmetics line. It's called Fit Me."

"That's what's up. I have heard of that. What's your mom's name?"

"Amira Summers. But most people know her as Amira Rochon."

"Name sounds familiar. It's cool she has her own company," she said nonchalantly. "So, what have you been doing since the last time we saw one another?"

"School, work and travel. The usual," he answered.

Two hours later they ended the conversation. It was the best time she had had in ages and not once during the entire call did he mention one thing about sex or make any sexual innuendos. She was impressed by him and that was not easy to accomplish. With the hard part of out the way, Kalia devised a plan of action.

Sebastian was different and if she wanted him to be her man, she was going to have to be different as well.

"Only a fool does the same things over again, expecting different results."

Kalia was many things, but a fool she was not. She picked up her phone and sent a 'thank you' text to Anika. If something good came of this, she would have to do something special for her.

All the years that Kalia had been knowing Anika, she never took the time to really sit and talk to her the way she did with Riley. Maybe that was because Anika never spoke about her family's wealth or possessions. Hell, the whole time they were in school, Kalia thought that Anika's last name was Pierce.

"I don't know where in the hell I got that from."

Had she known that she was as rich as she was, Kalia would have made Anika her primary BFF instead of Riley. Especially with the fine male cousins that she has. Either one of them would have been perfect for her. She was going to have to play her cards right with Anika to infiltrate the Rochon clan. Regardless of her friend's financial status, the friendship that they shared was genuine and not based on what Anika could do for her. Sadly, that wasn't the case with Riley.

Kalia had befriended her all those years ago based solely on her parent's wealth and Riley's generosity. It's not that Riley bought her friends, but they had so much money, it didn't matter what she spent and who she spent it on. This is what attracted Kalia to her. When she used to have sex with Ms. Lewis, the headmistress at Gateridge Prep, the administrator would supply her with all sorts of information about the other student's. Anika came to the school after Ms. Lewis left.

"It's good to have connections."

For the next few days, Kalia made sure to text Sebastian. Not long texts. Only enough to let him know that she was interested. It worked.

"Hey, Queen. It's Bash. How are you?"

"Better now that I'm talking to you."

"Listen at you. Quick question, do you like Beyonce?"

"Uh, yeah silly. Who doesn't?"

"You'd be surprised. How would you like to go with me to see her in concert'? I have front row tickets and two all-access back stage passes."

"Of course, I would. That concert has been sold-out almost a year. How did you manage that?"

"Bey is one of my mom's clients. She gave them to her."

"Your mom has the coolest job ever. I'd love to go with you. Can I ask you a quick question?"

"Shoot."

"Is this a....date?"

"It is. I plan on taking you to the concert and to dinner. Is that alright with you?"

"Yes. You can take me anywhere you want to. Sebastian Rochon, you are stuck with me."

"I don't mind that at all."

And so it began.

THE CLOSER I GET TO YOU

Sebastian Rochon had everything that Kalia required in a man. Intelligence, sexiness, and good looks. Most importantly he was wealthy and his family was one of the most prominent families in the United States. And he was all hers. Her hard work was paying off. Sort of. There was one last hurdle that she had to jump over. Sexing him. He was being too much of a gentleman. If she really wanted to secure her hold on him, she had to put it on him. And fast. It had never taken her this long to get anyone in the sack. If it wasn't for David, she'd have cobwebs on her pussy.

Thankfully, the pair was getting closer. That much was evident because today, they were at the Rochon Family Reunion Annual Black Tie Ball. It was the event that kicked off the reunion. This year, it was being held at the Westin Peachtree Plaza Hotel. The other events were going to be held at scattered sites around the city. They even had jet ski races planned at Lake Lanier during the week-long celebration. This was the first time she was going to meet his family. Including his parents.

"Why doesn't your mother host the family reunion at her estate? It's certainly large enough to accommodate everyone." She wanted to know.

"Because my cousin Pookie, steals."

They laughed.

"I'm laughing but very serious. The Rochon's are a motley crew. Stick around long enough, you'll see."

"I hope to be around long enough to find out."

"Play your cards right and you may. Come, let me introduce you to my parents."

Anxiously, she walked towards them. Amira Rochon was so regal she looked intimidating. Kalia was in awe of the multi-million-dollar mogul who stood before her. She had been a huge fan of hers for years.

"Ma, Pops, this is Kalia Hudson. Kalia, my parents."

"Hello," the young girl said nervously. "It's a pleasure."

"We've heard a lot about you, young lady and look forward to getting to know you better. You're just as lovely as Sebastian said."

Kalia gushed.

"Thank you so much."

They all stood around exchanging pleasantries before Bash whisked her away.

"Do you think they liked me?"

"I'm sure they did. If they didn't, they would have made an excuse to walk away. Instead, they talked to you and wanted to know more about you. You're a hit."

She preened like a peacock.

The D.J. slowed the music down and a lot of the old heads got up to dance.

"Warm night, can't sleep, too hurt, too weak, gotta call her up..."

If Con Funk Shun could get anyone on Love's Train, so could she. While she appreciated him being a gentleman, she was trying to see what he was working with between his legs. It was time for her to determine if he was worth scheming to keep. Who was she fooling? It didn't matter what size his package was. His family had enough money to buy a new one if he wanted to.

Her concern was getting him into bed and putting it on him so he wouldn't want anyone else. He was fine and wealthy and there were women young and old who wanted him. Since they connected, he had taken her on countless dates but they had all been innocent. Picnics in the park, fun at Six Flags, movies, dinner and dancing, you name it, they did it. Up until that point, he had only kissed her once and the kiss was something that he'd give a sister or close relative. Sebastian was a keeper and no matter how long it took, she was going to catch this fish.

So far, his mother and father loved her. That was half the battle won right there. The other relatives had warmed up to her and was already recognizing her as his girlfriend and that was also a plus. The side of Kalia that the Rochon's saw was sweet, hard-working, God-fearing and family oriented. All the things she was not.

"Let's dance," Sebastian asked when another slow record came on.

"Sure."

He took her hand and they weaved their way through the crowd. Sebastian and Kalia got out on the dance floor and he held her body close to his.

"I love this song, don't you?" He yelled over the loud music.

She was paying attention to him but still swaying with the music and every now and then her skirt rubbed against his pants. Sebastian put his hand on her arm and pointed out some of his relatives. The music cut just in time.

"Those are my two brothers, Xavier, the oldest and Bryson, the youngest. That's my step brother, James, that you met earlier. Anika, my first and favorite female cousin who you know quite well and Alexia, my annoying, yet loveable teenaged cousin."

"There aren't very many of you are there? My family is big. Between both of my parents I have at least thirty cousins."

"Darn it, that is a lot. We have lots of extended family but those are the ones who matter most to me."

"Darn it? Really? Aren't you an adult?" She said, mocking his choice of words.

Sensing an insult, he said, "so, the true sign of adulthood is cursing? I didn't get that memo."

"I'm sorry. I didn't mean to offend you. It's that I'm so used to hearing dudes cuss all the time I sort of expect it."

"First off, I'm a man, not a dude. You'll do well to remember that. And second, don't put me in the same box as the other losers you've known before. I'm not better than them, but I am different."

"Point taken. I do apologize," she said in elevated tones when the music started back.

They danced and talked until her feet hurt.

"Come on, let's go sit down and get you out of those heels."

At the table, he removed her shoes and placed her feet in his lap.

"I don't know why you women insist on torturing yourselves by wearing these things."

"Because we know you men love how we look in them."

"You're right," he giggled.

She wiggled her feet in his lap, connecting with his penis. On the dance floor, he could conceal his desire by keeping his groin away from her until it went down. Now there was no trick of the pants to hide his excitement and she looked up at him. Leaning in, he kissed her. Not lightly either. He kissed her with a passion and need he hadn't known was in there. She kissed back with a kind of urgent need that sparked him higher.

He took the wineglass from her and set it on the table then lifted her foot from his lap.

"Come with me."

Exiting the hotel ballroom, they made their way towards the elevators. The arrow lit up and they stepped inside the car. Sebastian pushed the button to the sixtieth floor. When she saw where they were going she started kissing him until she felt moisture between her thighs. He slid his hands up her hips and found no underwear so he cupped her ass and knelt to kiss her womanhood. They felt the elevator stop and he stood quickly. An older woman and her grandson stepped onto the car.

"Ahem." She cleared her throat, tilted her head and looked slightly down to the right.

"Pardon me," Kalia said, fixing her skirt that was lifted in the back.

A few floors later the people got off. Kalia and Sebastian burst into laughter.

"That was close. What are you trying to do to me on this elevator, Sir?"

"The same thing I'm trying to hurry up and get you to my room to do."

It seemed to take ages for them to arrive to their floor. Inside his room, he stripped off her shirt and put one leg up on the edge of the bed as he tasted her.

"Oh yes, Bash," she moaned as he drank her juices and felt her respond.

After the second time her knee almost buckled, he stood and pushed down his pants, stepping out of them and revealing his massive member. She stripped off her skirt, sitting on the edge of the bed and took him in her mouth. Sebastian caressed her body freely as she stimulated him until he pushed her off.

"Turn around, baby," he said and she got on her knees, laying her head on the bed. He entered her and they both groaned at the sensation. Slowly he began to move and soon was settled all the way inside her. He played with her breasts as they made love, then, when he felt he was getting overly excited, he paused and played with her body until she matched his excitement. Reluctantly, he pulled himself out of her and turned her over on the bed. Embracing her, he entered her as they kissed and rocked together. The measured strokes of his lovemaking culminated in an explosion of pleasure with them locked together, groaning and moaning.

"Damn, Kalia," he said, "that was intense."

"It was, baby, oh yes it was. But I don't want to give you the wrong impression, okay? This isn't like me at all. I like you, you are intelligent and fun to talk to. My plan was to get to know you better, not jump your bones like some slut. The last thing I want you thinking is that I'm the one-night-stand kind of girl."

"Shhh," he said and put a finger to her lips, "I am not either. Let's take it one-day-at-a-time, okay? On the dance floor, I sensed that you were feeling me as much as I was you. Was I wrong?"

"Not at all. I've never had such an intense attraction to any man ever. Honestly, you and I talked more today than I did the whole time I dated some guys. They wanted to fuck me and show me off. Instead of me being a trophy wife, I was a trophy girlfriend."

"I am the marrying kind. That's what the Rochon's do. I'm not saying that you and I are headed to the altar, but I am feeling you and would love to see where this can lead," he admitted.

"That is what I was hoping for, Bash. No matter what develops between us, we have our friendship."

She sounded so sincere that she almost fooled herself.

Smiling, he said, "My family has called me 'Bash' my whole life, but it has never sounded as sexy as it does coming from you."

"It's a sexy ass name. Sebastian Franklin Rochon."

"That's my name, don't wear it out."

"Your name isn't what I want to wear out." Caressing his dick, she massaged it back to life. "I've had too much wine to drive home. How long until we can do that again?"

"I'm ready whenever you are."

With her still lying on her stomach, he rolled on her backside and slid into her pussy. He made love to her until the effects of the wine had dissipated. She stayed by his side the entire week of the family reunion and they made love every chance they got before it ended. By the time she returned to work, Kalia felt as if she was floating on cloud nine.

A few months after the family reunion, Kalia decided that whatever she had to do to keep Sebastian she would. He had her sprung. Dating Colby had exposed her to so many different things and she thought she'd seen it all. Nothing could have prepared her for the life that Sebastian and his family lived. Even Anika. All of them lived so low-key. No one would ever guess that Sebastian was raised in a home that boasted eleven bedrooms and fifteen bathrooms. The house sat on ten acres and had everything that a person could possibly want. Except a full-time housekeeper and cook.

"I love cooking for my husband. There's no way I will allow another woman to *ever* feed my man," Sebastian's mother told her.

For the life of her, Kalia could not understand why Amira Rochon did not have any domestic help to take care of her home. Who cares who fed her man if he ate? If she and

Sebastian got married and they had their home built, it was imperative that they had staff to take care of it.

Since she had been dating him, Bash had not heard her utter one bad word about her family or the shack that she grew up in. As-a-matter-of-fact, any time that she spoke of them, it was always something positive and loving. He'd met her family as they had invited them over to Sunday dinner before. Her father loved him and so did her mom. Even her siblings got along well with him. Colby didn't want to be around her family at all. Especially her mom, citing that it reminded too much of the fact that his mother abandoned him.

Why am I thinking about that dude anyway?

Friday blew in like a tornado. Dr. Sutton's secretary, Lily, had worked every good nerve that Kalia had left. The woman was bitter, angry and alone. Everything Kalia hoped she wouldn't become. When Bash texted her and asked her out to dinner, she gladly accepted. He sent her a text and asked that she meet him at the restaurant. It was a new upscale soul food eatery with an excellent bar.

Although it was heavy traffic, she arrived five-minutes before their reservation.

He was standing at the entrance sending a text message when she walked in.

"Evening, Queen." He kissed her cheek.

"Hey, my love. How are you?"

"I'm good. Shall we go inside?"

The hostess escorted them to a private room in the middle of the restaurant. It was beautiful. Long burgundy drapes hung from floor to ceiling. Fresh white and pink roses were placed around the room in beautiful crystal vases. The room was romantic.

"Oh, wow. Pink and white roses are my favorite," she mentioned.

"Really? I'll have to remember that." There was twinkle in his eye.

"What do you recommend?"

"Everything is good here. Want to get a beverage first?"

"Yes-s-s, Baby. I need something stiff in my life and I'm not talking about a drink either."

He shook his head and motioned with his hand in front of his throat as if to say 'cut it out' but he didn't say it out loud. Clearing his throat he began to speak slowly, voice shaking.

"Kalia, you are an amazing woman."

"Thank you. I think you're an amazing man," she said, head down in the menu.

"When I first saw you at the graduation, somehow I knew we'd end up where we are now."

"Ah, that's so sweet. Do you think the oxtails are good here?" She asked.

"Woman, if you don't put that menu down," he scolded, pulling it from her grasp.

This was not going as he had planned. "Something big is happening here and all you're worried about is food." There was a giggle in the background.

"My bad. Did you laugh at me?"

"No, I didn't laugh at you."

"I could've sworn I heard laughter."

"May I finish, please?"

"Yeah. Sure."

"As I was saying, I knew we'd end up here. At least, that was my prayer. I had a talk with a wise man, the other day and he told me a story about how he met this wonderful woman and thought he'd play it cool and not tell her how he felt. He

229

thought he had time. But one day, she left and he didn't know if he was ever going to see her again."

"Did he ever see her again?"

"You're interrupting me."

"Sorry. Continue."

"He vowed that if he ever saw her again that he would tell her how much he loved

her every day for the rest of his life. Moral of the story is; seize the day."

"Awe, that's the sweetest story I've ever heard. Who told you that?"

"Your father, when he told me how he met your mother."

"When did you see him and why were you guys talking about that?"

"I went to ask him for permission."

Kalia picked up the menu and began scanning it again. This time, Sebastian didn't say anything. Instead, he got out of his chair and down on one knee.

"Permission for what babe?"

"To marry his daughter."

"Good for you, babe. To marry his daughter. To do what." She yelled, slamming the menu down. Tears welled in her eyes instantly when she saw him kneeling before her.

"You asked Daddy? What did he say?"

"I said yes, baby girl." Kyle Hudson said.

Kalia turned around and saw fifty people behind her. Her parent's. His parents. Her siblings. Even Justin. All his family. Anika and Riley. The gang was all there.

"Kalia Rae Hudson, your dad said yes I could marry you. Will you please do me the honor of saying yes to becoming my wife?"

"Yes. Yes. Yes. A million times, yes!"

And that's how she caught the biggest fish in the sea.

PRIVATE PRACTICE

"**V**agina's should come with a warning label. Caution, good pussy up ahead. Regrettably, they don't."

The young couple looked shell-shocked listening to their therapist. They were told that the psychologist had an unorthodox treatment process but they never imagined this. To begin with, their session was at night. What was even more peculiar is that currently, both of them sat on the sofa in the office, naked.

"Tell me, what seems to be the issue."

The petite wife began her explanation. "Well, we have been married for eight months and we are having some problems with - uh- intimacy. Not all of it only some parts. Mainly oral stuff."

"She's terrified of it," the husband added.

"I gathered as much. That's partly the reason why I have you guys undress when you come in. In this session, I need you all naked, mentally and physically."

"Dr. Hudson, I love my wife. I'm so busy now with work that it seems we're drifting apart in the bedroom. She's beautiful and sexy as hell in my opinion."

"Agreed. You two are newlyweds," Kalia began. "There's no way that the two of you should be able to sit next to one another naked, without wanting to touch each other."

"I'm a bit nervous. I've never been naked with anyone except for him. This is all so new to me," the young lady confessed.

"Trust me, I understand. The reason I wanted you two naked is because I want you to begin to explore one another's bodies, familiarizing yourself with every nook and cranny.

Chad, touch Jada's breast. Don't caress it, merely lay your hand over the globe."

He did as instructed. With no movement at all, Jada's nipple began to get hard.

"Wow. How did you do that?" Chad queried.

"It wasn't me. It was you and your wife. Sex is more mental than it is physical. Your thoughts about your wife and her thoughts about you should excite you to arousal. Now tell me, why don't you two like oral sex?"

"Well," Jada started. "I really don't mind doing him but I don't think I want him to do me."

"Why not?" If a man didn't eat her pussy, Kalia wasn't giving him any ass. It was a prerequisite for her.

"What if I taste funny?"

"The essence of a woman is delightful. Unless you haven't cleaned yourself, you should be fine. All women have their own flavor and smell. A suggestion that I've offered to other clients with similar fears is to lick a peppermint stick and insert it inside their vaginas. It will change your taste."

"I don't understand." The client looked very confused.

It was going to be one of those sessions.

"I like to guide my patients through demonstrations so they can face their uncertainties and fears. Let me show you what I'm talking about."

Kalia walked to her desk and took out a cedar box that contained candy. She unwrapped a peppermint stick and licked on it. Slowly, she let her tongue travel the length of the stick before sliding it in her mouth. Jada looked captivated at the therapist, wondering to herself how did the other woman learn to do that.

In the meantime, Chad sat with a hard woody, caressing his dick, imagining what his therapist's lips would feel like wrapped around his dick.

"Did you shave like I told you?"

Jada nodded.

"Open your legs," she commanded sternly. The client complied.

"I had you shave your pubic are for hygiene, to aid in instruction and to enhance the sexual experience. It is important for you all to know that I am STD free and if at all you feel uncomfortable with this therapy session, you can stop at any time."

Down on her knees, Kalia inserted the stick. Jada was moist enough for it to slide in. Holding it by one end, she swabbed her client's insides with it.

"Open your mouth," she told Chad.

When he did, she fed him the peppermint stick. He licked it, savoring the flavor of his wife mingled with the minty candy.

"Relax," she said.

She put her hands on Jada's knees and pushed her legs further apart. Tenderly, she licked the warm center of her beautiful client and began teaching her the joys of receiving cunnilingus. Kalia wrapped her lips around the hardened clit and began sucking on it gently at first and then applying pressure as she went along. Pulling back a tad, the naughty psychologist began stroking Chad's dick.

"Kiss your wife," she managed to say between licks.

He leaned in to kiss his wife who hungrily responded. The sensations coursing through her body were almost unbearable. Her legs began to quiver and Kalia pulled back. This time she moved.

"Your turn," she told Chad.

He rushed between his wife' legs, gripped her hips and pulled her to the edge of the sofa. Gazing at her glistening pussy until he couldn't hold back any longer, he buried his face deep. He started licking at her opening, wanting to taste every drop of the fluids his therapist had managed to create. Nibbling at each lip, he slipped a finger under her, so he could finger her backdoor. His lips moved to her rock-hard clit and he started sucking on it, making circles with his tongue, flicking it and nibbling, letting it slip between his teeth over and over so that she was moaning so loud neighbors would have heard them.

"Stop," Kalia commanded, pulling Chad back by his shoulders. There were juices around his mouth and in his thin mustache.

"Why, Doc. Jada was about to come," he protested.

"Which is why I had you stop. Follow me."

The confounded couple followed the therapist toward a back room that had double doors attached. She opened one and they found themselves inside a master bedroom suite. There were no lights on, simply the glow of flickering candles in the room.

"Get on the bed," Kalia told them. In one fell swoop, she pulled the wrap dress that she wore over her head and went to lie in the bed with them. "Jada, get as close to the headboard as you can and Chad you can get back between her thighs on your knees. I'm going to lie under you and suck your dick while you eat your wife out."

Chad went back to work and so did Kalia. He slipped a finger inside his wife, then another and started wiggling them and pounding in and out while he kept sucking, nipping and licking her hard clit. Finally, she came all over his face, screaming his name in pure ecstasy.

"Ooh, Chad. Don't stop," she sang out.

He lapped up every bit that he could.

"Fuck me, Chad," the therapist ordered.

Kalia was already on her back. Still frazzled from the powerful orgasm, Jada could do nothing but watch.

Swiftly, he penetrated her, turned on by seeing his dick disappear within her folds and she gasped and gripped his hips, pulling him all the way inside her. They moaned in unison, grabbing each other's asses as he started pounding her.

"Yes, that's it. Don't stop."

Not wanting to miss out on the action, Jada shifted in the bed and sat her pussy on Kalia's face. She gyrated in slow circles, rubbing her nub against her therapists' teeth.

"Mmm, this feels so good. I love getting my pussy eaten, Doc. Suck it baby." Jada had begun to loosen all the way up.

"Oh, yes. Give. It. To. Me. Chad." Kalia managed between his hard thrusts.

Knowing how much he was pleasing the doctor made him ram her harder. His thrusts were deep and intentional. In and out he stroked. One. Two. Three pumps and Kalia's body started spasming hard.

"Ahh, yes." She sang.

"I'm coming, Doc," Jada screamed.

"Fuck. Here it is," Chad chimed in.

They were all clinging to each other. Kalia's nails clawed his back, making him come harder. After they floated back to Earth and their breathing evened out, the psychologist got out of the bed and gathered her garments off the floor.

"I will leave you two to finish enjoying one another. There's a shower and garden tub in the bathroom. Feel free to use either one or both. I'm here as long as you all need me to be. Once you finish and you're dressed, come see me in my office and we'll talk about your experience."

The horny couple simply nodded.

"One more thing. Jada, put this on the base of Chad's dick. You can thank me later" Kalia threw a small package in the bed. It was a penis ring.

With trembling hands, Jada applied it to her husband's soft member before stroking it back to life. Afterwards, Chad pulled his wife to the end of the bed and rammed his dick deep in her pussy. On her way out of the room, Kalia heard her cry out in pleasure. An hour later, the couple knocked on her door.

"Come in, you two. How was it?"

Jada blushed. "Oh my gosh, Dr. Hudson, who knew that it could be that good?" The woman gushed.

"I did. And now I'm glad that you know, too. Take it slowly. Introduce new things in the bedroom one by one. I don't want you guys to get used to using anything other than your hands and bodies right now, okay?"

"We understand. Thank you so much for everything. Do we need to schedule another visit?" At two-thousand dollars a session? Of course.

"Yes. Osaphobia isn't a one session process. Depending on the client, it could be lengthy treatment."

The husband breathed a sigh of relief.

"We want to continue to see you. Jada was scared that this was our only session with you. Neither of us have experienced pleasure like this before."

"I'm here for you all whenever you need. I suggest monthly sessions with me, however, I would like you all to document things that you all do in the bedroom. There's no need to bring the journal in to me. This is for you all to go back and reflect on the things that you all like and don't like and how you can keep the fire burning in the bedroom."

"That's an excellent idea, Doctor. Again, thank you."

A knock came at the office door.

"Knock, knock."

"Hey, Sebastian," she greeted her man.

He saw the clients. "I'm sorry, did I interrupt your session."

"Not at all, we were finished. See you all next month."

"See ya, Doc."

"Thanks."

He waited until the door closed.

"Babe, I love how dedicated you are to your clients. You're an amazing doctor. And you smell so good," he said hugging her.

"Thank you, honey."

"Have you eaten?"

"A little," she replied slyly.

"Come on. Let me feed you dinner. Then later you can be my dessert."

"Ooh, la-la. Oh," she snapped her fingers. "Dr. Sutton said he wanted to talk to me about something important tomorrow. Do you think I'm getting a promotion?"

"I wouldn't doubt it. He's seen your hard work and dedication over the years. All of those long hours and hard clients have paid off."

She smirked at 'hard clients' because he had no clue how accurate he was.

"We'll find out tomorrow."

Before they left out of the office, she turned on the alarm and flipped the light switch. She'd had enough for one day.

☿

A practice of her own. That's what Kalia dreamt about for years. Not that she disliked working with Dr. Sutton. He was great. But anyone with an entrepreneurial spirit within them understood that if a person wanted to generate serious revenue and gain wealth, they would need to be their own boss. It's damned near impossible to become rich working for someone else.

"You will have offices adjoining these on the east-wing. Your private suite connects to this one."

"Oh, baby. Thank you so much. How can I ever repay you?"

Dr. Sutton rubbed his hard dick. "Climb on top and I'll show you."

Kalia slid her wet cunt down his pole and bounced up and down. He palmed her breasts and flicked her nipples with his index fingers making them erect. Using his thumb, he rubbed her clit, getting her worked up. Her vaginal muscles tightened around him and pulsated.

"Ayee, baby. I'm cumming."

Her juices flowed down his hard shaft and he released his hot seed inside of her.

"Married or not, this pussy is mine."

Married or not, this pussy is yours," she confirmed.

"And so is this," he said, positioning her on her side as he slid in her ass.

Kalia loved Sebastian but she would never stop fucking the doctor. Internally, she had to compartmentalize her sexcapades. Being with Dr. Sutton and clients was business. Being with Bash was pleasure. As she came again for the second time in a matter of minutes, she reveled in the fact that her business gave her so much pleasure.

IDO...DO YOU?

The final countdown had begun. Three weeks. Four days. Nineteen hours. Forty-seven seconds. That's exactly how long it would be before Kalia became Mrs. Sebastian Franklin Rochon. She would be the wife to a man who was joint-heir to a multi-million-dollar company. And they didn't have a pre-nuptial agreement. Could life get any sweeter? She looked at her sleeping fiancé and smiled, pulling the crisp, white sheet from over his body. With her at the helm of this ship, yes it could.

Kalia stared at his sexy, naked body. His dick was hard. She was fixated by it. Bash was still asleep but his member was wide-awake, rigid and throbbing. His gorgeous, engorged penis had a shine to it as it was stretched to its maximum length. She moved her hand towards his stiff meat. Closer. Almost touching. The palm of her hand was a fraction of an inch from his shaft. His dick quivered. Being that close to him created tension and an undeniable energy.

Shifting her entire body closer to his cock, she brought her mouth right up to the side of it and blew a soft, warm breath on it. She got on her knees, held her hair back and stuck her tongue out to barely touch the tip. It jerked slightly. She pushed her tongue into the slit of his head and gently twirled it around. Carefully, she allowed her tongue to travel the length of his dick and back to the top, gently sucking it and savoring it. Sebastian moaned but remained asleep.

There was a stiff, swollen membrane that was bigger at the base and thinned a bit as it went further up his penis. Her mouth moved to where his dick and balls met and she concentrated on sucking the base of his dick. Soft, slow circles were made and he let out a soft breath. Finally, she wrapped her soft hand around his firm member and began stroking it as she sucked. The blood was moving through his shaft and the persistent pounding of his pulse indicated that an orgasm was not far off.

Kalia kissed the head like it was her long-lost lover. She rubbed and sucked his dick until she felt him stir and awaken. Bash put his hand on her head and guided her as she made love to him with her mouth.

"Oh my," Sebastian said. "You look so good with my fat dick in your mouth, Queen."

Her long hair fell in her face as she looked up at him. Pushing it out of the way, she gave him a full view of her pretty face with his dick sliding deeper into her mouth. His dick was devoured with unbridled lust and fervor. The goal at hand was for her to extract every drop of cum from his massive balls and swallow every luscious drop of it.

"Oh fuck," he said, letting out a rare curse word. "Go for it, baby girl. Eat this dick, babe."

His excitement propelled her desires even more, encouraging her to suck and stroke harder. Moaning, she slid her finger between her wet slit and rubbed her own throbbing, engorged clit. At that moment, she wanted that nice big load of cum more than anything, hot and sweet, sliding down her throat. And she was going to get it.

Bash reached down and began playing with her nipples, rubbing them between the pads of his fingers. Her pussy was drenched. She was about to come. His body tensed up. Pulling her ass around so that he could reach her pussy, he began finger fucking her while she sucked his dick.

"Here it comes, Lia," he moaned. "That's it. Get it. Suck it, babe. Swallow it all." His hips bucked and lifted off the bed as he erupted and shot the hot load down her throat. It was so hot, Kalia felt the warmth of it inside of her belly. A few light strokes to her clit and she erupted in his hand. Juices ran down his forearm.

After their breathing returned to normal, he rolled over.

"Is this the way it's going to be after we are married or are you going to become a prude, wife?"

"Husband, it's only going to get better from here. If you think this is good, you have not seen anything yet."

"I hope so. Hey, my estranged father reached out to me after ten years of no physical contact. He wants to have lunch. Should I go?

"What do you mean no physical contact?"

"He provided financial support. My college tuition was paid in full before I left junior high school."

"Whoa. Your dad is doing it like that?"

"Yeah, but money isn't everything."

"Rurghh," Kalia uttered sounding like Scooby-Doo. To her money wasn't *everything*. Money was the *only* thing. "I think you should hear him out. Never know how things will work out."

"True. Come on, Queen. We must meet Mrs. Amira for some last minute wedding details. Let's get ready. Your mother-in-law hates tardiness"

For the next couple of weeks, the couple stayed busy. Work and wedding planning didn't mix. Today they were headed to Centennial Park to shoot the first of many engagement photos. They had already had a few taken but it wasn't enough for what Mrs. Rochon had planned.

Kalia basked in the fact that they didn't have a budget. She wanted to gloat and rub Kennedi's face in it but it wouldn't have done any good. Her sister was too busy enjoying impending motherhood. Something that she may never have the chance to experience. Any time she and Bash talked about kids, she told him that she wanted as many as he did. The bride-to-be wasn't the only one thinking about children because no sooner did they arrive at his mother's home; did she bring it up.

"Hey honey bunches of oats," she said to her son, hugging him first, then her future daughter-in-law. "You two have no idea how happy I am about this wedding. Hopefully, and you know I've been praying about it, I'll end up with some grandchildren. That's the only thing this house is missing, the pitter patter of little feet."

"We're going to start asap, mom. Me and my boo have already had some conversations about it. Haven't we love?" He said kissing her check.

"Yes, ma'am. Both of us want children," she lied with a straight face.

There was no way she was going to let kids ruin her figure or her relationship. Kids made things worse, not better.

Mrs. Rochon and Kalia's mother worked together to make sure the last minute details were ironed out. Atlanta's top rated event and wedding planning agency, Total Elegance Events and Planning was handling everything and they were doing an excellent job. However, Mrs. Rochon didn't want to leave anything to chance.

Like Kennedi, she was able to wear an Andell Original Fairytale gown and she was stoked. The staff at *All About Her Bridal Boutique* treated her like a celebrity. She was pampered and fawned over like she was Beyonce. This is the way Kalia felt she should have been treated her entire life. She was caught up in a whirlwind of happiness.

When all was said and done, every flower was in place. Every decoration was hung. And the meal was cooked to perfection. It was time for a wedding. Kayla was chosen to be Kalia's maid of honor because she was the first friend she'd ever had. She had fifteen bridesmaids that included Anika and Riley. It was one of the largest weddings the city had seen. The ceremony was held at Chestnut Hall. The largest, most expensive home in Atlanta. Everything was perfect.

"Daughter, I want you to know how very happy I am for you. You finally found your Prince Charming among the sea of frogs."

"Thank you, Mommy."

"Here, this is for you," Riley said. She put a pretty, yet subtle diamond tennis bracelet on her friend's wrist. "Something new."

Mrs. Rochon stepped up and put a diamond necklace around her neck. "This was my great-great-great grandmother's. I think it's pretty old and it's also borrowed," she finished.

"Well that pretty much covers it all then," Kalia said happily.

"No, it doesn't. You forgot something blue," Riley observed.

"Not at all. Anika took care of that first. Kalia pulled the bodice of her gown down enough to reveal the powder blue, lace strapless bra she had on. "I've got the matching panties also."

"It's time baby girl," Kyle Sr. said. "Are you ready?"

"As I'll ever be."

He kissed her cheek and led her out of the room.

Everything went by in a blur. Kalia zoned out everything else except Sebastian when she saw him looking so handsome at the altar. She and her father literally floated down the aisle to the Wedding March. When he surrendered her to Bash, Kelli got up and serenaded them with her newest single, "A Love That Lasts Forever." The song ended as beautifully as it began and the wedding program commenced.

So many loud thoughts raced in her head. She heard every other word the preacher said. The preacher was speaking in such a dull, monotone voice, like the preacher at her sister's wedding. Had she not been standing, she would have passed out from boredom.

"...not to be entered into lightly."

The first thing I'm going to buy is a house." She thought. She couldn't believe it. In a few minutes, she was going to be Mrs. Sebastian Rochon.

Eat your heart out, Kennedi, she thought inwardly, looking out toward where her sister sat. *I'm going to be richer than you.*

The beautiful bride looked at her groom with hope. Their smiles almost brighter than the future that they hoped to have together.

"...and if anyone should object to this, speak now or forever hold your peace."

"I object!"

It was a voice she recognized. Slowly she turned around to see who it was. There was a man at the back of the room, coming down the aisle with an angry stride. Before she fainted, she got a good look at the opposition. It was Nelson Franklin.